SHOWSTOPPER

She looked bewildered as the full spotlight came back to her and the applause broke loose. She bobbed a curtsy, swiftly, awkwardly, still glancing around like a wild, frightened thing. Then she dashed offstage.

The amplifiers went on, the beat loud, solid, hypnotic, for Black Bart's entrance.

'Homesteader, Homesteader,
    Ridin' alone . . .'

His face was black and thunderous as he strode on. She had killed his enterance, and he knew it. There could be only one sad and lonely principal in the act. She had stolen the mood and part of it had exited with her.

Once again, there'd be hell to pay when the public performance was over. No wonder she had wanted to stick to comedy.

AGATHA CHRISTIE

Death on the Nile
A Holiday for Murder
The Mousetrap and Other Plays
The Mysterious Affair at Styles
Poirot Investigates
Postern of Fate
The Secret Adversary
The Seven Dials Mystery
Sleeping Murder

DOROTHY SIMPSON

Last Seen Alive
The Night She Died
Puppet for a Corpse
Six Feet Under
Close Her Eyes
Element of Doubt
Dead on Arrival
Suspicious Death
Dead by Morning

ELIZABETH GEORGE

A Great Deliverance
Payment in Blood
Well-Schooled in Murder
Coming soon: A Suitable Vengeance

COLIN DEXTER

Last Bus to Woodstock
The Riddle of the Third Mile
The Silent World of Nicholas Quinn
Sevice of All the Dead
The Dead of Jericho
The Secret of Annexe 3
Last Seen Wearing
Coming soon: The Wench Is Dead

MICHAEL DIBDIN

Ratking

LIZA CODY

Stalker
Head Case
Under Contract

S.T. HAYMON

Death of a God
Death and the Pregnant Virgin
A Very Particular Murder

RUTH RENDELL

A Dark-Adapted Eye
  (writing as Barbara Vine)
A Fatal Inversion
  (writing as Barbara Vine)

MARIAN BABSON

Death in Fashion
Reel Murder
Murder, Murder, Little Star
Murder on a Mystery Tour
Murder Sails at Midnight
The Stalking Lamb
Murder at the Cat Show
Tourists Are for Trapping

DOROTHY CANNELL

The Widows Club
Down the Garden Path
Mum's the Word

ANTONIA FRASER

Jemima Shore's First Case
Your Royal Hostage
Oxford Blood
A Splash of Red
Quiet as a Nun
The Cavalier Case

MARGERY ALLINGHAM

Police at the Funeral
Flowers for the Judge
Tether's End
Pearls Before Swine
Traitor's Purse
Dancers in Mourning

COVER-UP STORY

Marian Babson

BANTAM BOOKS
NEW YORK · TORONTO · LONDON · SYDNEY · AUCKLAND

This edition contains the complete text
of the original hardcover edition.
NOT ONE WORD HAS BEEN OMITTED.

COVER-UP STORY
A Bantam Crime Line Book/published by arrangement with
St. Martin's Press

PRINTING HISTORY
St. Martin's Press edition published 1971
Bantam edition/November 1991

CRIME LINE and the portrayal of a boxed "cl" are trademarks of Bantam Books,
a division of Bantam Doubleday Dell Publishing Group, Inc.

ISBN 0-553-29330-3
Published simultaneously in the United States and Canada

Bantam Books are published by Bantam Books, a division of Bantam
Doubleday Dell Publishing Group, Inc. Its trademark, consisting of the
words "Bantam Books" and the portrayal of a rooster, is Registered in
U.S. Patent and Trademark Office and in other countries. Marca
Registrada. Bantam Books, 666 Fifth Avenue, New York, New York 10103.

PRINTED IN THE UNITED STATES OF AMERICA
RAD   0 9 8 7 6 5 4 3 2 1

CHAPTER I

THE PRESS CONFERENCE was going well—as Press Conferences go. The Fleet Street boys were lit up, the Client wasn't. Their initial efforts to trap him into some incautious quotations had been sidestepped and they were past caring now. His latest LP was booming out over the amplifiers with a hypnotic beat, and the Press Release was so well written—if I do say it myself—that any sub could dredge a few hundred salient words out of it when his principal staggered back to the office.

For the moment, it looked as though I could relax. I snatched a Martini as the tray went past and retreated into a corner where I could keep an eye peeled for trouble.

It was the wrong corner and trouble was waiting for me. 'That room you got for Lou-Ann—' Maw Cooney had been lurking behind the drapes—'won't do at all. I never saw such a poky little hole in all my born days. Are you sure this is a high-class hotel?'

I took a deep swallow before replying. She'd done nothing but complain since she stepped off the boat-train. 'It's generally considered to be one of the best hotels in London.'

'I'd hate to see the worst!' She sniffed and glanced

sharply at the glass in my hand. 'Young man, are you supposed to be drinking on duty?'

'I'm a Public Relations Officer, Mrs Cooney—not a policeman.' To underline this, I took another swallow. You have to assert your independence with some of these characters. And she wasn't paying my salary.

'You haven't answered me. What about Lou-Ann? The Good Lord knows I don't mind for myself—I could sleep on a heap of rags in a corner—but it's a question of the fitness of things. Lou-Ann *is* the comedy star of this Troupe, after all, and it's mighty kind of her to agree to double up with her dresser—but to ask *two* of us to share that teensy little—'

'I'll see what I can do, Mrs Cooney,' I interrupted her. 'In fact, I'll see right now.' I got away quickly before she could block my retreat.

This corner was an improvement. There was nobody here but us chickens. It was clear now that the crowd was beginning to thin out a bit.

The LP hesitated, then began on the big one—the Top of the Charts—the number that had lifted Our Boy right out of the boondocks and into the big time.

　　'Homesteader, Homesteader,

　　　'Ridin' alone . . .'

You could call it Ballad, Country & Western, or Folk Music—whatever was 'in' this year. The music was plaintive, the lyric melancholy—and it had touched a chord in a lot of people. It was about a homesteader who had fenced off his acres, then had to fight beef barons who reckoned they owned the grazing rights to every acre of God's whole creation; just as he was wearying of the struggle, they cut a hole in his fence and stampeded the cattle through; his wife and the child she was about to bear were killed, and now they'd never drive him away because all he had was buried here on this homestead, and he'd stay until they buried him here, too. The Client was alleged to have written it himself—and it sounded semiliterate enough to be possible.

'*Homesteader, Homesteader,*
    '*Ridin' alone . . .*'

Uncle No'ccount moved forward slowly, pulling his harmonica and a red bandana from his hip pocket. He spat his upper teeth into the bandana and stowed it back in his pocket. He wrapped his lips around the harmonica and breathed into it. A cold wail of melody whiffled a chill down every spine as he picked up the tune.

He was every bum who'd ever hopped a midnight freight, one jump ahead of the railroad police, on his way from nowhere to nowhere, gone too long from home to even remember what he was running from any more.

'*Ridin' alone now,*
    '*For ever alone . . .*'

Cousin Homer chimed in softly with the guitar and Cousin Ezra took up the plaint with the fiddle. They seemed okay, although a bit too awkward and gangly, with wrists and ankles dangling too far out of their clothing for their ages. If they'd done any growing since they bought those clothes, they ought to will their bodies to the Harvard School of Pathology. Still, the fans hadn't seemed to notice—and who was I to knock a successful routine?

They were all playing along with the record now. If the Client held out much longer, it was going to be pointed. I looked over to try to catch his eye.

I needn't have bothered. He was already moving front and centre, grinning his lazy grin, forelock down over one eye, gliding with easy catlike grace. The grin didn't reach his eyes. The reluctance in his shrug was real—the self-deprecation wasn't. I'd only known this crew for six hours, but already I had enough of the picture to realize that there was going to be hell to pay for this performance—after the Press had left.

They'd reached the echo chamber bit when he took up the tempo. He looked more like Black Bart the Last of the Bushwhackers than Bart the Lonely Homesteader; but this was the act that was paying off, so this was the act he was doing—or almost.

The echo chamber did a little to disguise it, the live music did the rest, but Black Bart wasn't singing. His timing was perfect, the graceful throwaway gestures fitted perfectly. He stood there, miming to the record and, except for the musicians, I was probably the only one to notice it. It confirmed my opinion. The Client wasn't giving anything away free.

    'Homesteader, Homesteader,
     'For ever alone . . .'

The spattering of applause showed how far the party had gone towards breaking up. During the number the waiters had been moving around purposefully, removing empty glasses from tables and detaching near-empty glasses from hands. Ashtrays were being emptied, and a couple of old-retainer types were doddering forward from the far end of the room, managing, like ancient collies, to herd the strays along in front of them.

The Client patted a few shoulders as they passed. 'Nice to have met y'all,' he said. 'Sure hope I'll be seeing a lot more of you.'

His eye had been resting on someone's little office junior as he said that, and I got a nasty feeling that it had a double meaning. At the very least. We were being paid far too much for this job—there must be some deep jagged icebergs beneath the glittering tops that broke the surface.

The last of the Press, exiting, collided with Lou-Ann, entering. She squawked and hurled herself back against the door frame. They glanced at her curiously, but Crystal Harper was right behind her, and nobody with all their hormones operational was going to waste time looking at Lou-Ann when Crystal was around.

Maw Cooney swept down on Lou-Ann, scolding, 'Where've you been? All them reporters were here—and they were taking pictures, too. Now you've missed the whole thing. And you, the comedy star!'

'Sorry, Maw,' Crystal Harper said, with lazy indifference, 'I'm afraid we went shopping and didn't notice the time. Girls will be girls, you know.'

Maw Cooney flashed her a look that told her she'd never been a girl. Several unmentionable variations, perhaps, but never *that* kind of girl.

Over Maw's head, Crystal met the Client's eyes. *He* wasn't complaining. It occurred to me that it might have been deliberately engineered that Lou-Ann miss the Press Reception.

Lou-Ann whirled around and began babbling apologies to the Client. He nodded, not really looking at her. 'It don't matter. You're all right, honey.'

'But I missed *everything*. Now they won't have any pictures of me,' she wailed.

'You go talk to the Publicity Boy,' the Client jerked a thumb at me. 'He'll fix up something. That's what we're paying him for.' He gave her a shove that was rough but—for him—probably not unkindly, and she stumbled towards me.

* * *

She was the kid next door who had grown up, taken the braces off her teeth, thrown away her glasses, had her hair curled—and then found out that it *still* didn't make any difference. So she'd decided to play it for laughs. Sometimes they make worse decisions.

Somewhere between the shopping tour and the Press Reception, she'd climbed into her trade mark 'comedy costume'. The high-necked long-sleeved blouse bunched itself out of a low-necked short-sleeved red jacket with half the buttons missing. The rusty black skirt dipped to several lengths and multi-coloured patches had been sewn at random on it. The straw hat had two large daisies drooping from broken stalks and was moored precariously to the top of her head by an elastic string passed under her braids.

The freckles scattered all over her face were probably real and not painted on. She smiled at me nervously. There was lipstick on her front teeth. I didn't think that was an intentional part of the costume—she was just the sort who always would have lipstick on her front teeth.

'I'm sorry,' she said. I had to lean forward to hear her. 'I should have kept an eye on the time, but it was so excitin' bein' here, and seeing all those famous stores—'

'Don't you go apologizing to *him*—he should apologize to *you*.' Maw Cooney had come up behind us with the battleflag flying. 'You're paying him—it was his job to keep those reporters here until you arrived. Stars are *expected* to be late. How dare he start before you got here?'

Lou-Ann looked up at me. She'd been chewing gum. Now she pursed her lips suddenly and broke into a broad grin, goggling her eyes at me. It was liquorice gum, and she'd blacked out her two front teeth. On the whole, I preferred the lipstick.

But I recognized it as another form of apology, this time for Maw Cooney, so I nodded and smiled at her, and she relaxed.

Over her shoulder, there was a performance going on in the second ring.

Black Bart had come up behind the musicians as they were settling down their instruments. When Uncle No'ccount pulled the bandana containing his upper set from his pocket, Bart snatched it away.

'You stupid no-account old fool!' He balled his massive fist around the bandana and shook it under Uncle No'ccount's nose. 'What do you think you're playing at? Know what I ought to do? I ought to stomp on these for you!'

'Aw, now, Bart, don't take on so.' Uncle No'ccount kept his eyes on his uppers. 'We didn't mean no harm.'

'You never mean no harm—but you go and do it just the same. Listen, when I decide we'll do a Benefit, *I'll* give the word!'

'Sure, Bart, sure. I just got kinda carried away. Didn't mean to upset you none—did we, boys?'

The Cousins shuffled their feet and shook their heads, miserable at being appealed to. Only too obviously, they had been hoping to remain unnoticed and escape involvement.

'We was just funning, Bart.'

'No call to take on like that, Bart.' They spoke together, backing towards the door.

' 'Tweren't like a for-real show, anyhow, Bart,' Cousin Ezra said. 'You know we ain't wired up right yet for this neck of the woods.'

'That's right, Bart,' Cousin Homer chipped in. 'That fella there said he was gonna see about it, but he ain't done nothing yet.'

That sent the ball swinging into my court.

'You, boy!' Black Bart shouted at me. 'Hump it over here and let's hear what you got to say for yourself. How come you ain't got my boys fixed up yet?'

Uncle No'ccount reached out and gently removed his belongings from Bart's hand while he was distracted. A quick flourish of the bandana and his teeth were firmly where they ought to be. He beamed with relief and straightened his shoulders, standing taller.

'Reckon I'd better get along and tend to some unpacking,' he said. 'You don't need me for this. One thing about a good old harmonica—you cain't fit wires to it.'

'Okay, but you just watch it, you hear?' Bart glared, but the menace was wasted on Uncle No'ccount's back, so he turned it on me.

'You don't move very fast round these parts, do you, boy? We told you as soon as we got here an' took a look at the electricity to get the plugs changed an' slap transformers on all the instruments. S'pose I shouldn't be surprised it ain't been done yet, now I see how long it takes you to even cross a room.'

It was a pity Perkins & Tate (Public Relations) Ltd needed the money so badly. It would have been a pleasure to tell him what I thought of him and walk out.

On second thought, I probably couldn't tell him anything he hadn't heard before. And we needed the money. He might be a bastard, but he was a solvent bastard.

'I put in a call for an electrician,' I said. 'They promised to speed it up and have one over here first thing in the morning. That means some time tomorrow afternoon.'

He glared at me suspiciously, but seemed to realize I was serious. 'Hell! What a country!' he exploded. 'I got thousands of dollars worth of electronic equipment here, and it ain't worth a damn unless I can get the juice going through it.'

'You'll have everything ready in time for your opening,' I said. 'You've only been in the country about eight hours, why not relax and enjoy it?'

'You trying to be smart, boy?'

'We had to skimp the introductions to get ready for the Press,' I said. 'My name is Perkins, Douglas Perkins.'

'Like I said, you trying to be smart, *boy*?'

The Cousins began to snicker, then to push each other about. 'You hear that, *boy*? Yes, sir, *boy*!' They scuffled wildly.

'All right, cut that out!' They had brought unwelcome attention back to themselves. 'You got off light— *this time*. Don't let it go to your heads.'

'Yeah, Bart.' 'Sure, Bart.' They were instantly subdued.

'You got nothing better to do—cut along to your hotel and get some more practice. You flatted that top note on me. Do that on stage and you'll be swimming back home the hard way—under water.'

They slunk away quietly, but before I had time to enjoy the peace, Maw Cooney was on us.

'Young man, have you got that room changed yet? By rights, we ought to have a suite. You can't expect Lou-Ann to put up with being treated like poor white trash.'

Since that was what she'd gone to great trouble to dress herself up to look like, it would seem to be an occupational hazard. Perhaps that was why Maw Cooney, as her dresser, was so sensitive about it.

'*You* tell him,' she whirled on Bart. 'Lou-Ann is the comedy star of this Troupe. She deserves better than that poky old room. There isn't room enough to swing a cat in there. Tell him we want a room befitting her position.'

You had to hand it to her for bravery, if not sheer gall. They were lucky to be in the same hotel as the Great Bart. Uncle No'ccount and the Cousins had been salted away over in the heart of 'Europe On Five Dollars A Day' territory. But, obviously, Maw Cooney was not one to sit back and count her blessings.

Bart turned his head slowly to stare down at her. I closed my eyes. I hate to see a man hit an old lady— no matter how much she's been asking for it.

When I opened them, she was still standing there, untouched. Bart's eyes had narrowed dangerously, but he hadn't said a word.

'You tell him now.' She insisted on crowding her luck. 'You order him to find a nicer room for Lou-Ann. You know it's due her—in her position.'

Crystal had moved up behind Bart and, once again, an unspoken communication passed between them.

Suddenly, Bart shrugged. 'Right, Maw.' He glared at me. 'See to it, boy!' He jerked his head at Crystal and they left the room together.

Maw Cooney fussed her way back to collect Lou-Ann. On their way out, she stopped to say, 'We'll pack our things. We didn't unpack much, anyhow, once we saw that awful place. You get the bellboy to move us. We'll be out getting a bite to eat.'

I stared after them thoughtfully. After a moment, a throat being cleared over by the door brought me back to the scene.

CHAPTER II

SAM MARCOWITZ. Now there was a man who could give wallpaper lessons on fading unobtrusively into the background.

All this time he had been sitting at the table by the door, thumbing through the Guest Book the Press had signed as they arrived.

I walked over to him. 'What's a nice boy like you doing in a place like this?'

'Honest to God, mister,' he whined. 'I never done nothing like this before. You're the first. Why don't you sit down and have a slug of booze while I slip into something more comfortable.'

He reached under the table and brought out a bottle of scotch the waiters had neglected to reclaim, and loosened his tie. 'Jeez, what a blast!'

I had gone to school with his elder brother, Nathan. Twice, in fact. Once when Nate had come here as part of the 'Junior Year Abroad' scheme of his American college and attended my Redbrick university. And the second time when I had taken a postgraduate course at the Harvard School of Business Administration. After which, we had spent a year together in one of the lesser-known Madison Avenue advertising agencies.

Nate had gone onwards and upwards with the almost-arts and was now climbing into the top executive class at one of the really important agencies. I had come back to England—it had seemed like a good idea at the time.

But she had married a Title with money attached, while I was still trying to get my feet under me. That set my feet properly loose, and I took off for the Continent. I met Gerry Tate while we were both doing a stint for Cinecittà in Rome. We decided that, since we could deal with the paparazzi, we ought to be able to manage Fleet Street, where the natives were at least friendly.

Since he was one of the wrong Tates, it took a while to earn enough money to start out on our own. And that was where Nathan Marcowitz had come back into the picture. We had corresponded casually. I sent scrawled postcards from wherever I happened to be, and he sent back secretary-typed notes giving me the latest Trendex Ratings on his commercials. What the hell, it kept us in touch.

The week after I'd broken down and written a real letter—I was younger then, by about a hundred years—outlining our plans for Perkins & Tate (Public Relations) Ltd, a cheque arrived. He wanted to buy in as a sleeping partner. Every smart young business exec should diversify. I thought he must be joking, but the cheque didn't bounce, and we were in business.

That was two years ago. So far, Perkins & Tate were still eating, but Marcowitz hadn't had any return on his investment. Not only that, he'd had to kick in with a couple of thousand more dollars to settle an unavoidable overdraft. I'd been wondering for some time just when he was going to get tired of writing us off on his income tax return as a loss.

Now, here was Brother Sam with Black Bart and the Troupe—a nice fat account dropped into our laps, with only a week's advance warning by cable. This could be it. A big Stateside build-up behind the Client, with a guaranteed fee. Let's see you muff *this* one. Little Brother is watching.

I freshened my drink from his bottle. Hesitated, when I noticed his eye on my glass, then poured more in. That's not the answer, Little Brother. If the firm goes bankrupt, it won't be because Perkins & Tate are secret lushes. We don't need a gift subscription to Alcoholics Anonymous, just an introduction to a good tough collection agency.

'How *did* you get mixed up with this bunch?' I really wanted to know. Perhaps it would give me the answers to a few other questions.

'I don't remember. Suddenly, everything went black and, when I came to, they told me I was their Road Manager.'

'And this is the Road?'

'This is the Pie in the Sky. The roads they were on before, they didn't have to have a manager. Bart and the Troupe just played it by ear as they went along. They got paid off in black-eyed peas and ham hocks— or anything else they considered negotiable.'

'But then they hit the Big Time.'

'Yeah. Frankly, this is the problem.' He became serious, leaning forward and giving me that straight, sincere look with which Ivy League graduates preface their shiftiest deals. I knew that whatever was coming next was going to be from the bottom of the deck.

'They hit it before they were quite ready. So we thought we ought to groom them a bit before we give them the full treatment.'

'We?'

'They've signed a Television Contract. One of Nathan's clients is going to sponsor them on a weekly half-hour, coast-to-coast, next season. But everybody agreed they could use a little more polish first.'

'So they shipped them off to England, hoping some of our Olde Worlde culture would rub off on them?'

'That's right. Nathan and the Agency decided I ought to come along as Road Manager, since I knew something about Show Business to begin with. I guess you could say I'm really holding a watching brief.' He smiled with sincere insincerity.

So, Little Brother was watching all around. That much I believed. In fact, I believed all of it. So, why did I have the feeling that I'd just been dealt a hand full of jokers?

Perhaps it was the way he was looking at me—or not looking at me. He met my eyes only occasionally, in that straightforward look, then his focus shifted abruptly, as though, having scored a point, it had better things to do. Mrs Marcowitz hadn't brought her boys up to be good liars.

I'd never forget the Thanksgiving Dinner I'd had at their home. Mrs Marcowitz had been carving the turkey (the old man hated the job) and we had all been talking. Sam and Nate had been reviewing one of the plays in the football game that afternoon. 'And how about that dumb centre-forward?' Nate had said. 'Anybody who couldn't have blocked that pass, Jesus—' The flat side of the carving knife descended sharply across his knuckles. 'We do not take the name of God in vain in this house,' Mrs Marcowitz had said, and waited. 'I'm sorry, Ma.' Still, she waited. Nathan glanced around the table. 'I'm sorry, everybody, I apologize.' Satisfied then, Mrs Marcowitz had gone back to the carving. She had brought her sons up to be gentlemen, in the best tradition of the American Dream. She wasn't to know they'd be taught a different dream at those schools she'd scrimped to send them to. They had worked out their own version of the American Dream now, but they were going to be slightly handicapped in achieving it—early training dies hard.

'I was rather surprised you brought them over by ship,' I said. 'I thought air was the only way to travel these days. Time is money—and all that—especially while they're still at the top of the Hit Parade.'

'Yeah, well—' Sam's eyes danced off to survey the horizon—'I'll tell you the truth.' Another bad sign. 'They've been working awfully hard lately. Series of one-night stands from Nashville to Tuskaloosa and back again. We figured they were overtired. A nice sea voyage, six days on the ocean, give them a good rest and a chance to get themselves into shape to face new audiences over here.'

Maybe—just maybe—managers, out of the kindness of their hearts, were sending artists on sea voyages at the height of their drawing power because they might be overtired.

'One more thing,' I said. 'What does your mother think of this crew?'

'Ma? She doesn't know them. It's nothing to do with her.' Sam stood up, his eyes steely. 'You'd better go and get those reservations changed for Lou-Ann, hadn't you? There'll be hell to pay if you don't.' He turned and walked out.

So, now I knew. They weren't the sort of people you brought home and introduced to Mother. Well, I'd mixed with some characters at Cinecittà that *I'd* be happy never to see again, let alone introduce to my mother. But, somehow, with the Marcowitzes, it meant something different.

And there was one other little thing that bothered me about Sam these days—his hands. When I'd known him in the old days, he'd worn fingernails.

I was very thoughtful as I made my way to the desk clerk. Handling Black Bart and the Troupe might be very good for the Perkins & Tate bank account, but I wondered if we might wind up crying all the way to the bank.

I arranged for Lou-Ann and Maw Cooney to be transferred to a double room on the sixth floor. Which reminded me—there was one other member of the Troupe. A second guitarist with a stomach ache. I'd better get over to *their* hotel and check on whether it was just a memory of mal-de-mer, or whether he needed a nice National Health appendectomy. All part of the service.

I dropped off the bus at Bloomsbury Square and cut through Russell Square. Behind an unprepossessing Edwardian front, the lobby was full of tourists queuing to cash travellers' cheques, or to ask if there was any mail. I sidestepped them all and joined the crush waiting for the lift. I was able to push my way in on the second trip and, firmly pinioned between two blue-rinsed ladies, I heard far more than I ever wanted to know of the details of Susie's operation. I broke free at the third floor, just as the surgeons were leaving a sponge inside, and walked up the remaining flight.

The sound of the harmonica guided me down the hallway. A shoe-box at the end of the corridor had been allotted to Cousin Zeke, and that was where I found them all. It was quite a homely little scene.

In the traditional manner of friends cheering the sick all over the world, the others were crowded into the room, going about their business, ignoring Cousin Zeke, who was lying there looking greyer by the minute—as well he might.

Uncle No'ccount was leaning against the wall, whuffling softly into the harmonica. The plaint was unfamiliar, but melodious, perhaps some old American country ballad. His eyes were abstracted and he was paying no attention to the others.

Cousin Homer was sitting on the edge of the bed, paring his toenails. Actually, I was rather relieved to see this—I gathered it meant he wouldn't be doing it onstage. After witnessing Uncle No'ccount and the bit with the teeth, I wasn't sure just how far they went. On the other hand, if they unbuttoned sufficiently, there was a sporting chance they might be taken up by the Sunday critics and become a rage with the intelligentsia.

Cousin Ezra, sprawled in the room's only armchair, was engrossed in a magazine. I was surprised to discover he could read but, looking closer, I saw that it was a girly book. That was more typical.

They became aware of me suddenly. The harmonica died to a moan. Uncle No'ccount whipped it from his mouth and, for a moment, looked as though he were going to hide it behind his back. Cousin Ezra closed the magazine and sat on it. Cousin Homer wavered, but must have decided he was the only respectably engaged one of the lot. 'Evenin',' he said, quite civilly for him.

'Good evening,' I said. 'How's the patient?' Cousin Zeke opened his eyes, but the effort of focusing was too much, and he closed them again. I began to get worried. Seasickness wouldn't have lasted this long. He should have had his land legs under him by this time.

'He's feeling a mite poorly, still,' Uncle No'ccount said unnecessarily. He glanced at the closed door. 'You come along by yourself, did you? Nobody waiting outside?'

'I'm alone,' I reassured them. 'I thought I'd look in and see how you're settling in, and find out whether there was anything I could do for you.'

Cousin Ezra snorted, wriggled the magazine out from under his rump, and went back to memorizing the blonde on page 12.

'Nice of you. Mighty neighbourly.' Uncle No'ccount nodded amiably at me, and the harmonica crept back towards his mouth.

'Mighta knowed it,' Cousin Homer said. 'Y'all didn't think Bart was gonna come slumming just 'cause Zeke was sick, did you?'

'Like to see him show up here.' Cousin Ezra looked up balefully. 'We're on our own time. He comes shoving his nose into this hotel, I'll tell him what he can do.'

Oh, yes. The cat was away, and the mice were flourishing flick-knives and bragging to each other about how they were going to take him next time he appeared on the scene.

'About Zeke.' I tried to call the meeting to order. 'Does he seem better or worse than he was on the ship? I mean, do you think he needs a doctor—or have you already sent for one?'

They thought I was mad. It was in every expression. Even Zeke propped one eye open to regard me with a jaundiced look.

'It will be safer to have a doctor check him,' I persisted. 'You're booked for your first show day after tomorrow. You want him to appear, don't you?' A delicate thought occurred to me—I wasn't sure how much they were paid, but I'd received the distinct impression that Black Bart wasn't exactly the last of the Big Spenders. 'You don't have to worry about the money, you know. We have a National Health Service, it won't cost you any—'

I stopped short. They were laughing at me. Not loud honest laughter, but the half-audible snickers that told me I had run afoul of a long-standing situation I knew nothing about. It was in-joke laughter, and I was on the outside looking in. Perhaps they'd explain it, so that I could join in the laughter, and perhaps they wouldn't. I waited.

'Hell, boy!' Cousin Ezra exploded. 'He ain't *that* kind of sick.' They burst into guffaws. 'He's sick, all right, just like he's always been. But it's all in his head. It's all some kind of psycho— psycho—'

'Psychosomatic,' Uncle No'ccount clarified. It wasn't until later that I thought the word surprising on his lips. 'That poor boy's always like that—every time we travel. Seems his ma took him to a Conjure Woman when he was a-growing up, and that Conjure Woman, she told him he was gonna die away from home. So, every time he gets away from home, he's like this for the first two-three days. It wasn't so bad when we was starting out, but it's been blue murder since we got famous and been doing those one-night stands all over the place. Some nights, he's got up on that stage with so many pills inside him, we wasn't never sure he could even stand up, never mind play music.'

I looked at them suspiciously, but they were serious now. 'You don't mean it—no one believes in Conjure Women in this day and age!' I was trying to convince myself, however. If anybody believed in that sort of thing, *this* little lot would.

'We don't know as he really believes it,' Cousin Homer said, 'but he just ain't *sure.* He'll be all right after two, three days, though. When he sees he's still alive.'

'Be all right now,' a voice from the bed said weakly, 'if I could just have my pills.'

I looked at Uncle No'ccount, but he shook his head. 'Nope,' he said. 'Bart threw his tranquillizers and sleeping pills overboard. Said he was sick and tired of all this foolishness. Kill him or cure him, Bart said, and he didn't care which, but he'd had enough of this damnfool nonsense.'

For the first time, I felt a fleeting sympathy with the Client. It couldn't be easy trying to work with this bunch of morons, no wonder he had such a nasty temper. It wouldn't do my own temper any good if I had to have much to do with them. But it was only for six weeks and, I reminded myself, Perkins & Tate needed the money.

'Bart'd never've knowed—' Cousin Zeke surfaced

again, to glare accusingly at Uncle No'ccount—'if Maw Cooney hadn't of snitched to him.'

'Yeah,' Cousin Ezra joined in venomously, 'she never could mind her own business. Somebody oughta take a meat axe to that old bag.'

'Trouble is—' Cousin Homer seemed to be peacemaker—'she reckons Lou-Ann would take over that extra number if Zeke falls down on the job.'

'She oughta—'

'Easy, boys, easy.' I decided I ought to try some peacemaking myself. At the same time, it was all grist to the mill. The story of a Conjure Woman and a hexed musician was a colourful one—perhaps we could get some coverage out of it. Build up some suspense about whether Cousin Zeke could pull himself together enough to appear on opening nights. Would the show go on, in the Great Tradition—that sort of thing. Carefully, though, we'd have to lose the part about the pills going overboard. The idea of big, kindly, lonely Homesteader Bart destroying a sick man's medicine wouldn't do anything for *his* image.

'I'll see what I can do about getting some more tranquillizers,' I promised. 'And I ought to talk to Bart, too. Do any of you know where he is?'

'Out on the town, way he always is when we hit a new place.' Cousin Ezra's mouth quirked slyly. 'With Crystal.'

'And Lou-Ann,' Uncle No'ccount said, studying his harmonica.

'And Maw Cooney,' Cousin Homer added. He glanced obliquely at Uncle No'ccount.

Once again, there was a private joke in the air. Even Cousin Zeke, who had given up trying to keep his eyes open, was lying back on the pillows with a knowing smirk on his face.

Once more, I was on the outside looking in, trying to assess what the hell was going on. Uncle No'ccount and Maw Cooney? Why not? It took all tastes. She wasn't a bad-looking woman, if you didn't mind the battleaxe variety.

With a show of indifference, Uncle No'ccount began improvising on the tune he had been playing earlier. The Cousins were openly grinning now, watching me challengingly. Inviting me to ask more questions, to start the hare running. There was a lot they could tell me that I ought to know, their attitudes implied.

No doubt there was, but I had had a long hard day. Whatever the Facts of Life among this troupe, I could learn them some other day. And, preferably, from some other people.

'Since there's nothing more I can do for you, I'll say good night now,' I told them. If I'd been in the right mood, I might have found the looks of disappointment on their faces, as I closed the door behind me, comic.

But I was in the wrong mood. I didn't like any of it. The uneasiness I had felt all day was stronger than ever. Something very unpleasant was coming—and nothing could stop it.

I was going to find out the Facts of Life, all right. But I wasn't going to go looking for them. Not with the Cousins.

They were the kind of nasty-minded little boys Mother had warned me never to go behind the barn with.

CHAPTER III

⊒

I WENT BACK to the office. Perkins & Tate (Public Relations) Ltd have a small office flat near the top in one of the buildings sloping down towards the river in Villiers Street. If Maw Cooney had ever seen it, she'd have thought her old room was the Grand Ballroom at Buckingham Palace by comparison.

Gerry Tate was brooding at the window, fouling the atmosphere with one of the tiny cigars which were trying to fool the public that they were non-carcinogenic cigarettes. We had held that account for a month before the client decided one of the big advertising agencies could do a splashier job for him. We still had a crateful of the product under the desk. When we were desperate we smoked them, but we'd never again mention them by name. No publicity once the client has withdrawn the account. I saw five stubs in the ashtray. The situation must be serious—Gerry wasn't even making a face as he inhaled.

'Which account did we lose this time?'

He hadn't heard me come in. He jumped, but recovered quickly. 'I always said we ought to stay out of the art game.'

That was his story today. He'd been the enthusiastic

one when the lady sculptor approached us a month ago and suggested that she was willing to pay a modest amount in order to get as much publicity as possible for her first one-man show in thirty years.

We'd done all we could, but she'd hated most of our ideas. Gerry had wanted her to jazz up the show by scattering a few urinals, tastefully decorated, of course, among the general works. He'd pointed out, quite rightly, that it was the sort of thing that got critics enthusiastic these days. We'd nearly lost her then and there. She was a serious, solid lady, and her works were serious, solid figures of Earth-Mother types—the sort of thing that had had a brief vogue in the thirties. But she was sure that she had 'something to say' to today's audiences. The show had opened this afternoon, while I was trying to get Black Bart and the Troupe from the boat-train to their hotels, and then on to the Press Conference.

'What happened?'

'She lost her temper.' He turned away from the window. Three long jagged scratches ran down the side of his face. 'I guess it took her by surprise, but she'd never have agreed if I asked her.'

I waited.

'Well, you *know* it's the only way to get space these days. You know that Earth-Mother in the—uh—unfortunate position?'

Practically any of them could be described that way, but I thought I knew the one he meant. I kept waiting.

'I hired a bidet from a plumbing supply company and shoved it under the statue.' He raised his hand and stroked the scratches gingerly. 'The boys loved it. The show will be in most of the papers in town.'

'But we won't get paid for it.'

'Well—uh—no. While I was trying to hold her off, I gathered that we were not only fired—we'd never been hired. But she'll be written up on the news pages, instead of being tucked away in a couple of art reviews.' He brightened. 'Maybe we could sue?'

He was a nice guy. He tried. Most damning of all—he meant well. Usually, I liked him. A feeling of great weariness descended on me and I slumped into the chair behind the desk.

'Hell, Doug—I'm sorry. I didn't know she'd take it like that. I know this is a hell of a time to have this happen. With the sleeping partner's brother in town, and all.'

And all. And maybe ready to take over Perkins & Tate; to step in as boss and show us how to run the company. Why not? He could scarcely do worse.

'Arrrgh! I don't know why we keep trying!' Gerry stubbed out the cigar, reached for another, and drew back. 'People are always saying, "Where are the Great Press Agents? Why don't we have publicity stunts like they used to have in the Good Old Days?" '

He was the only one I'd ever heard saying that, but I just nodded. He'd read all the books about the Good Old Days. They'd gone to his head.

'But I say, "Where are the Great Clients?" They're all gutless wonders these days. They think reporting a jewel robbery is the way to get their names in the papers. Where are the Clients who'll put their shoulders to the wheel and co-operate? Where are the Clients who'll dress up in an Admiral's uniform and review the Fleet? Who'll cross Niagara Falls on a tightrope today?'

'Blondin was a tightrope-walker to begin with,' I put in.

'Gone, all gone,' he shook his head sadly. 'Now they hand you a mug shot beaming over a birthday cake or an engagement ring and expect you to get headlines for that. Or a baby. How the hell can you get a four-column cut for a bratling, after the first shot with doting mummy in hospital?'

It was a good routine. Perhaps Sam would be impressed by it. It isn't our fault, it's the Client's. Everybody's out of step but Gerry and Doug.

'Oh, well,' Gerry sighed, and raised his hand solemnly. 'Never, never again, do we mention the name of that hyphenated-hag. No free publicity for her, ever.'

I raised my right hand. 'Never again.'

'Enough of my troubles,' Gerry said. 'How did you get on with the Homebreakers—or whoever they are?'

Despite the cheery front, his morale was too low for the truth. It might do me a world of good to confess my uneasy feeling that Black Bart and the Troupe were going to join the ranks of the Great Unmentionables—after doing us a lot of damage first—but I had to consider the business.

'Okay,' I said.

Because of my connections with Sam and Nate, I was to be liaison man with the Troupe. Gerry was to hold down the office and take care of any other assignments that might float in. He wouldn't be able to do his best if he were wondering when the axe was going to fall on me.

'Thank heavens that's one place we've got an *in*,' Gerry said soberly. 'Marcowitz has them all tied up, and they can't sack us—or refuse to pay.' He was brightening by the minute. 'Treat 'em gently, Doug, they're our meal tickets for the next six weeks.'

Before turning in, I tried to call Sam, but the hotel said he had gone out with Miss Harper and her party and they hadn't returned yet. That didn't surprise me. From the little I'd seen of Crystal Harper, I'd figured her more for Sam's type. But I wondered how Bart would like the competition tagging along. If he reported unfavourably to Nathan, we might not have Little Brother watching us for long. It was a thought to cheer me briefly.

In the morning, I managed to contact Bart, who sounded none too happy at being disturbed at the crack of dawn—otherwise known as eleven a.m.—and put my idea for a few paragraphs about Zeke and the Conjure Woman to him. He wasn't delighted at the thought of anyone else in the Troupe getting any publicity but, after half an hour, he reluctantly agreed, probably just to get me off the phone.

After that, I did some fast telephoning, then scrawled a longhand Press Release for Penny to type when she came in.

After that, it was time for me to show willing at rehearsal.

It wasn't the Palladium, but it had its points. It was close to the centre of London, it had a good stage with decent acoustics, and it had been available. It also had a large auditorium—and we'd be lucky if we could fill it and keep it filled, particularly in view of the short notice Gerry and I had had of the imminent arrival of America's Newest Sensation.

Sam was standing at the far side of the stage, talking to Crystal and Lou-Ann when I arrived. The Cousins were rehearsing centre stage, and I wondered how they had become so popular—even as a backing group. And how Sam was going to tone them down for American television. I had the nasty feeling that the way they were gesturing with those guitars was part of the routine and, while it might get by on BBC-1, any American television station would black out the act. They like to keep things pure and untainted for the Bible Belt and family audiences over there.

Sam was looking nervous, perhaps because Bart was standing nearby glowering at them all. Crystal was ignoring Bart—a little too obviously. Lou-Ann, in 'comedy costume', kept darting sidelong glances at Bart.

Uncle No'ccount leaned against the wall, midway between Bart and the girls, whuffling softly into his harmonica, paying no attention to anything going on around him. Just an old no-account bum doodling musically until it was time for his cue.

But he was the one who greeted me, who bothered to murmur that Cousin Zeke was feeling better now that the doc had seen him and would probably be all right for the opening, although not feeling up to the strain of rehearsals. Then he seemed to feel that he had done his duty, his eyes glazed over with a distant look and he went back to his harmonica. I walked over to join the others.

Sam nodded to me absently, then went on with what he was saying. 'Just *try* it straight. Just once. I tell you, it's a mistake to hoke it up after that introduction.'

'I don't think I ought to change it,' Lou-Ann said doubtfully, 'it always gets good laughs.'

'That's the point—you don't *want* laughs with that number. It isn't right.' Sam sounded hoarse, as though the argument had been going on for a long time. Lou-Ann looked unconvinced.

'Leave her be,' Bart broke in. 'Let her get the laughs—it's what she's here for. If you want the number to stop being funny, then give it to me to do. Or maybe Crystal.'

There was a nasty silence, during which I had the illusion of watching wheels within wheels—all going round. I hadn't much doubt about what Crystal did, and now it seemed she was going to be pushed into the act. Did that mean Lou-Ann, the 'comedy star', was in the process of being pushed out?

'I don't think so,' Crystal said. She had a nice voice, but it held the ineradicable twang of the Ozarks, betraying her inevitable beginnings in some hill country cabin. Somewhere along the line, she'd been educated, perhaps even sent to finishing school. But the finishing school hadn't been one of the top-flight ones, and it had still been too far south of the Mason-Dixon Line. The Ozarks were in her voice to stay.

'What do you mean?' Bart snarled.

'I don't want a number,' Crystal said. 'I don't want to be part of the act. I don't want to go onstage.'

'You shut up!' Bart raked her with a lazy, proprietorial glance. '*I'll* tell you what you want.'

'Things better stay the way they are,' Lou-Ann said. 'We know where we stand, then.'

'You think so, huh?' There was menace in Bart's darting look, and it stayed when he turned the look back to Crystal. 'Where were you later last night?' he demanded. 'You weren't in your room.'

'She was with me, Bart,' Lou-Ann cut into the awkward silence quickly. 'In *my* room. We were playing gin rummy.'

Bart looked at them both suspiciously. 'I didn't know you were so fond of gin rummy.'

'Sometimes the notion takes me,' Crystal drawled.

'Yeah?' He still wasn't sure whether he could believe them, but they were presenting a united front. 'Sure musta been an interesting game. I kept calling your room about every ten minutes till way after two in the morning.'

'You should have called *my* room, Bart,' Lou-Ann said softly. Her face was wistful. Bart ignored her.

'There goes your cue,' Sam said in a tight voice. 'You'd better get on stage.' His face was dead white, he didn't look directly at anybody.

So *that* was where Crystal had been last night! No wonder Little Brother was falling down on his watching brief. He was too busy playing with fire.

With Bart onstage, Uncle No'ccount put away his harmonica and moved closer to us. He gave Lou-Ann a meaningful little nod—at least, it must have meant something to her. She flushed and smiled slightly.

Sam had turned to face the stage, still pale, with slow fury smouldering in his eyes. I began to wish I hadn't bothered to come this morning. This set-up was worsening every time I saw it. My sympathies were with Sam, of course. Even if we hadn't been friends from away back, I'd have been on anyone's side against Black Bart.

'Looks like you have your hands full,' I said to him. Onstage, the Cousins were gesturing with their instruments again.

Sam winced and nodded glumly. 'Nathan wants me to get the act more sophisticated before the Agency shows it to the Client. He wants the boys to be more like the Sons of the Pioneers, and less like sons of bitches.'

'Then why didn't—'

'We need a photographer.' The evasive note was back in Sam's voice. 'To be on duty for a couple of weeks. Snapping candids. For the fan magazines back home.'

'That can be arranged.' Gerry didn't have all that much to do, and he was good with a camera. 'I'll bring one along to the opening.'

'Fine.' He didn't sound happy; but, like me, he probably wouldn't be until this assignment was over and Black Bart was just a memory to haunt our nightmares on dark and stormy nights.

Meanwhile, we were blocking the way. Lou-Ann had to push past us to get on to the stage. Sam caught her arm as she passed and looked at her searchingly.

'I can't.' She pulled herself free. 'Bart wouldn't like it. He wouldn't like it at all. You heard him.'

Sam lost the colour he had been regaining as we watched her stumble onstage. She took a pratfall and sat there, the broken daisies bobbing wildly on her hat. Cousin Homer came forward and, with exaggerated courtesy, pulled her to her feet. She overbalanced and flew past him, offstage into the wings on the other side.

There was a flat pause, probably filled with a laugh during the actual performance. She gave it a count of five, then staggered back onstage, eyes popping, mouth open. It was overdone.

Women shouldn't be knockabout comics. I'll grant them equality in everything else, but they sacrifice too much when they compete in that field. A few have managed it, but they've had enough finesse to work some pathos into their acts, and enough femininity to make sure of at least one scene where they appear in full glamour regalia. All the cards were stacked against Lou-Ann, and it wasn't fair.

'Come on,' Sam said abruptly, 'we don't want to watch this.'

I followed him backstage. Crystal and Uncle No'ccount were watching silently from the wings as we passed.

'Wait in the dressing-room,' Sam said. 'I just want to have a word with the electrician.'

He hadn't said which dressing-room. I by-passed the first one, with a big gold star—the Client would have appropriated that. There were three closed doors beyond that, with no name plates, and I was playing 'Eeny, meeny, miney, mo,' when one of them opened.

'Come in, young man,' Maw Cooney said. She was brandishing a late edition, which boded no good. 'I've been thinking you and I ought to have a little talk.'

Short of straight-arming her and rushing through the Stage Door to daylight and freedom, there was no escape. I meekly went into the dressing-room, hoping Sam would find me—and find me quickly.

She shut the door firmly behind me—if she'd shot the bolt, I would have gone straight through the window on the other side of the dressing-room. Fortunately, she didn't.

Locked or unlocked door, the lady made me nervous. Especially when she gave me that phoney smile. I recognized the newspaper as one which was carrying a column filler on Cousin Zeke.

'Now, you know I ought to scold you,' she said, still with that unnerving smile. 'Here's Lou-Ann, the comedy star of the Troupe, and you go getting publicity for one of the backing group. I ought to be good and mad and truly light into you for that!'

'It was a nice little story,' I said, keeping a wary eye on that rolled newspaper.

'Well, I can give you some wonderful stories about Lou-Ann,' she declared. 'I mean, I've decided that's where we've been going wrong—you and me—we haven't had a real good heart-to-heart talk. Why, you don't know what material you've got to work with. Sit down!—and let me show you!'

She had backed me up against a chair and I collapsed into it as she snapped the command at me. Where the hell was Sam?

'That's better.' She discarded the newspaper and went to get something from the dressing-table. For a moment, I thought she was lugging a suitcase over to show me. Then I realized it was a pile of the damnedest scrapbooks I had ever seen. They were made of black and white cowhide, with rawhide thongs, and Maw Cooney was staggering slightly under the weight. If the whole troupe carried those sort of things around with them, no wonder they had come by ship. Just one would have taken up their entire baggage allowance by air.

'You just look at these, now.' She slammed them down on the table beside me. 'Ain't they grand? There's a story right there in them alone. They was a gift to Lou-Ann from an admirer. Yessir, a lonely cowpoke made them himself for Lou-Ann after he heard her sweet voice on the radio. Wanted to marry her, too, he did—sight unseen. Of course, we had other plans, but he took it real well and sent her the scrapbooks, anyhow.'

She pulled one forward and opened it. 'You look at this now. That's Lou-Ann in her first appearance. At the Palace in—well, you wouldn't know the place. It's not a big town, even for Tennessee. But Lou-Ann took first prize in the Amateur Night there. Twenty-five dollars she won, and she came in second in the Finals, too. She won a weekend for two in Atlanta, Georgia. My, those were exciting days. But we knew it was just the start of her career. And she's worked. Lordy, how she's worked!'

Incredible as it seemed, Lou-Ann had improved from her earliest days. Her teeth almost fitted her face now, and her eyes, although still enormous, looked more as though they belonged to her, too. Her taste in clothes hadn't improved, though.

'And this is Lou-Ann the time she was guest star on Grand Old Opry,' Maw Cooney continued. 'Do you know, she drew more fan mail than Minnie Pearl? Mind you, I'm not saying that was the reason she didn't get asked back again—' she pursed her mouth and nodded sagely at me—'but the *public* went wild over her. Of course, I know she was only contracted for one appearance, but wouldn't you think they'd have signed her up after a response like that?'

For a dresser, she was pushing pretty hard. I looked at her again, studying her thoughtfully—something I had never been able to bring myself to do before—and there began to be something terribly familiar about those slightly protuberant eyes and the set of the jaw. A slow penny began the long slide towards dropping.

'Now, here,' she turned another page, 'is Lou-Ann on the day we went for her screen test in Tallahassee. My, she was wonderful in that. She was just as good as Sarah Bernhardt would have been. But, do you know, we never heard anything more from them. If you ask me, they didn't even have any film in that camera. I don't believe that was what they had in mind for Lou-Ann at all. But you should have seen their faces when *I* turned up along with her.' She sniffed. 'I sure enough put a spoke in *their* wheels.'

I shot an arrow in the air. 'Lou-Ann is certainly a lucky girl to have a mother like you to look after her interests.'

'And she knows it!' Right on target. 'We've seen too many little second-raters drifting around, not knowing where they're going. I made up my mind there'd be none of that for Lou-Ann—she's going straight up to the top. She'll be on television in New York next season, you know.'

I nodded. Stage Mother. I should have spotted it before, but there had been such confusion in the hasty arrival that I could excuse myself for not having picked up all the relationships.

It was another problem to brood over, however. Perkins & Tate had never handled that sort of thing before. One of our friends had. He'd picked up a Stage Brat, complete with Stage Mother, about a year ago. His hair had been jet black then—we called him Tinsel Top these days.

'And this one.' She was still turning pages, and we weren't halfway through the first scrapbook yet. There were three of them, and a smaller one at the bottom of the pile. If Sam didn't collect me soon, I wasn't going to last out the afternoon.

'What's that one?' I asked, more to divert her than because of any curiosity, pointing to the smallest scrapbook.

'Oh, you don't want to see that one,' she simpered, pulling it out before I could agree with her. 'It's just a little one that's all *my* work.'

She flipped it open. It was pasted up three columns to a page, with a picture of Lou-Ann heading each column, beside the caption: 'SEE THE STARS—WITH LOU-ANN MARS.'

'I been doing this four years now,' she said. 'It's syndicated in six fan magazines. 'Course, I make out like it's written by Lou-Ann herself, but she'd never have time to do it. It's all about the wonderful places she goes, and the famous people she meets, and how they're just like you and me really. You'd be surprised all the fan mail she gets about it.'

At this point, nothing would surprise me. 'Mmmm-hmmm,' I said, making the fatal mistake of actually reading a couple of sentences my eyes had carelessly rested upon. They were larded with the sickening cracker-barrel philosophy Americans specialize in, and lightened with alleged jokes that were older than Joe Miller. I turned a page hastily.

'Matter of fact,' Maw Cooney said, 'I was working on our first column from London, England, when you came along.' She reached for a heavily ruled pad and I knew that, if I didn't get away, she was going to read me selected snippets—perhaps even the whole thing. I set the scrapbook down and began sidling towards the door. The hell with waiting for Sam—in a situation like this, it was every man for himself.

'I wanted to ask you—' she whirled, and her gimlet eyes halted my hand halfway to the doorknob—'how do you spell Olivier?'

'What?' I said.

'*You* know,' she said, 'Sir Olivier. I thought it would be a nice touch in the column if I had Lou-Ann meet him and he kissed her hand and said what a wonderful actress she was.'

Stunned by the mental picture, I spelled it automatically and this time succeeded in getting the door open.

'Where are you going?' she demanded. 'You haven't seen the other scrapbooks yet. They're full of ideas.'

Happily, I had one myself just then. 'I'm going to arrange for a photographer,' I said, truthfully enough.

'There now!' she crowed with delight. 'That's more like it. I just knew seeing all about Lou-Ann would inspire you.'

'That's right,' I lied cravenly, and gained the corridor.

'You run along now,' she said. 'And let me know when you want Lou-Ann. We always co-operate with the Press just as much as ever we can.'

'Fine.' I closed the door behind me, but didn't bother looking around for Sam. I needed a drink and, in any case, I had the distinct feeling that he had forgotten me.

Anyway, I consoled myself, it could have been worse. She could have wanted to know how many l's in Philip.

CHAPTER IV

BACK AT THE OFFICE, there was no sign of Gerry, either. It was possible, of course, that he was with one of our other clients. Gerry always rang around first thing in the morning to count our chickens and find out if any hands needed holding during the day. He usually turned up a palm or two. At last count, we still had the dubious privilege of representing two 'resting' actors, one film producer on the run from the bailiffs, a company director with a burning urge to have every sneeze reported in *The Financial Times*, a radio actress currently appearing in an off-Broadway comedy in New York, and an Italian restaurant. At least we ate regularly.

We might eat even better, if we managed to keep Sam happy. I looked around the office and paranoia set in—Sam was probably on his way here right now, and the place looked like a badly-appointed pigsty. I ought to try to clean it up.

I removed a pair of Gerry's dirty socks from the filing basket and another pair from the Pending tray, rolled them together and pitched them into his room. It was a start, but the place still looked fairly squalid.

Emptying the ashtrays helped, but not enough. I was

collecting cups and saucers from the windowsill when Penny came in. She smiled at me, glanced around the room, and got the picture immediately. 'Having a tidy-up, are we?' she said.

'We may be having visitors any minute. Lend a hand, will you?' The request was unnecessary, she had already picked up the filing basket and headed for the files.

'New client?' she asked hopefully. She was always cheering for us.

'Road Manager for Black Bart and his Troupe,' I said.

'Oooh, good!' She finished the filing, pulled a duster out of the bottom drawer and began running it over the furniture.

She was a lovely kid. Just turned fifteen, she had left school last term and was currently serving time at a secretarial college in the mornings. She came to us afternoons and Saturday mornings, practised her shorthand and typing, made our tea, did the charring and any other odd jobs that came up—and seemed happy about the whole thing.

In return, we paid her six pounds a week, and let her bask in the glamour of it all. It was too bad that, inevitably, some busybody would explain to her about money, and we would lose her.

Meanwhile, the place was looking better already. 'Good girl,' I said, rather as though she were a bright puppy. 'Good girl.' She was more like a kitten, though, all fluffy hair and enormous eyes, overbalancing on long spindly legs. She'd be a beauty in a few years, but we wouldn't see it—unless she took it into her head to come back and see if we were still keeping out of bankruptcy court. Or perhaps—I tried to look on the bright side—

perhaps our luck would change, and we would be able to afford to give her a raise and take her on full time when she finished college.

'I heard the record—"Homesteader",' she said. 'It was on the radio yesterday. I'm going to get the record for myself on Saturday. It's wonderful. Is—will—' The words were tumbling over each other. She stopped and tried again.

'Do you think Black Bart would autograph the record for me? He *will* be coming in here some day, won't he? Do you think I could meet him?'

'Why not?' Another instalment of the glamour of it all. Something to tell her friends about. I hoped Bart wouldn't disillusion her too badly. He seemed to be canny enough to wait until the Press got out of the way before throwing any scenes. If I could slip Penny in with a Press party and get her out again before Black Bart reverted to type, she ought to be able to have her little thrill and keep her illusions intact. 'We'll see what we can arrange,' I promised.

'Wonderful! Oh, thank you!' I might have promised her the Taj Mahal by moonlight. She went back to her typing with renewed enthusiasm.

I took the seat behind the desk and started to look busy, prepared for Sam to walk in and discover us both hard at work.

It was a good pose and, when I looked at my watch after actually finishing off what work there was, I discovered that I had held it for over an hour. Sam had had plenty of time to get here, even if he had walked. Americans, however, take taxis if the distance is farther than twenty yards. He should have been here long ago.

That uneasy feeling was creeping over me again. I reached for the telephone and tried the hotel.

I got through to Sam directly. 'Where the hell have you been? I thought you were coming here, after I missed you at the theatre. I want to see you.'

'Yeah, sure, Doug, I'm sorry. I tell you, I was coming over there, but I got sidetracked. Couple of other things came up. You know how it is.'

'Well, are you coming over now?'

'I'm sorry, Doug. I'd love to, but it just isn't possible right now. Too many things to attend to. You know how it is.'

I didn't, but I was beginning to find out. 'Perhaps I could come over there. We ought to have a talk, you know, before I can do much more about the Press before the opening.'

'Yeah, I know that, Doug. Sorry, you'll have to play it by ear. I'll tell you, I'm not going to be at the hotel this evening.' His voice had a shifty note in it. If we were face to face, I had the feeling that he would refuse to meet my eyes.

'It's kind of awkward right now. You know how it is when you get to a strange city, and I've got all these people to look after. Honest, Doug, I don't have a spare minute today.'

I hung up thoughtfully. One thing had become quite clear in the course of the conversation. I should have been relieved. Instead, I found that it only added to my uneasiness.

Far from watching me, Little Brother was actively avoiding me.

* * *

Just in case no one else was covering the Opening, Gerry borrowed a flash camera. On the way to the theatre, we picked up Penny, festooning her with bags of spare flashbulbs and plates, so that she'd look useful and, possibly, even like a member of the Press.

We pushed our way through what looked like a crowd of hired extras (perhaps Sam had pulled himself together enough to give Perkins & Tate an object lesson in publicity) in the foyer and went backstage. It was about as hectic as I'd thought it would be, and no one was paying any attention to us.

I tucked Penny away in a corner of the wings, where she'd have a good view of the show, left Gerry beside her with instructions to keep the flashbulbs popping throughout the performance, and went round to the dressing-rooms to see if the troops needed cheering.

It was strictly a one-stop journey. I'd noticed before that the Cousins believed in communal living. This time they were spread out all over the corridor outside Black Bart's dressing-room. His door was open and I could see Crystal and Lou-Ann inside. Maw Cooney knelt at Lou-Ann's feet, sewing an extra bright red patch to the seat of her skirt. Behind her back, Cousin Ezra panto-mimed a hearty kick at her rear. Charming. And typical. I was glad I'd left Penny in the wings.

'I thought I'd drop by and say "Good luck",' I said.

'That's mighty neighbourly of you.' As usual, Uncle No'ccount was the only one who bothered with the little niceties of life. The others looked at me with mild curiosity and some distaste, as though I might have crawled out from under some log best left undisturbed.

Then Cousin Ezra seemed to decide that he ought to be cordial, too. 'Howdy, Doug Boy,' he held out his hand.

Like a fool, I took it. A jolt of lightning bit into my palm and travelled up my arm, to the accompaniment of a buzzing noise.

'Haw! Haw! Sure enough got you that time!' Cousin Ezra fell about. The others snickered merrily.

'That Ezra—he's a one!' Maw Cooney said, twisting round to smirk up at me. 'You got to watch him every minute. He's a real practical joker.'

I rubbed my aching palm. 'I can see that.'

'Where the hell's Sam?' Black Bart was *not* amused and called us to order. 'He oughta be here. And what the hell are *you* doing?' He had whirled on the unfortunate Cousin Zeke.

'Nothin', Bart, nothin' at all.' Cousin Zeke had been gulping a handful of pills. He put his hand behind his back.

'You better be doin' nothing. Just you let me catch you doin' something, and there's gonna be trouble like you never seen before.' He turned away abruptly.

Cousin Zeke snaked his hand back to his mouth and gulped a few more pills. I reflected that my doctor was reputable and a shrewd psychologist—the pills were probably nothing but placebos. At the rate Cousin Zeke was downing them, even aspirin would be dangerous. No wonder Bart had confiscated his pills, if this was the way Cousin Zeke took them.

'You make a better door than window.' Bart shouldered past me. 'If you ain't got nothing better to do than stand there gawping, why don't you go away?'

'Good idea.' I mentally withdrew any good wishes I had extended towards him. 'I'll go out front and watch the show. I haven't seen it yet.'

'I'll come along,' Uncle No'ccount fell into step beside me. 'I oughta be getting onstage. I open the show, you see.'

I saw. It fitted in with the rest of the picture. Any nasty job, anything hard, tricky, any spot where a person might fall on his face—went to anybody in the Troupe except Bart. The Client wanted his path made straight for him, and he got it. I wondered fleetingly if they were all in such desperate need of money that they had to put up with that kind of treatment.

To my surprise, they had the beginnings of a good show, even before Bart made his appearance. The curtains parted on a vaguely Western set, suggesting a barn, corral and watering trough. Uncle No'ccount was leaning against the corral fence, oblivious of the audience, softly playing the harmonica to himself. For a moment, all you got was the feeling: the isolation, the longing, the haunting distant something. Then I recognized the melody, it was the old Spiritual 'Lonesome Valley', but Uncle No'ccount's harmonica gave it an extra dimension.

I noticed the telltale flash from one side of the stage and winced inwardly. Gerry was taking his directions too literally. The Client wasn't going to be happy about flashbulbs being wasted on anyone but himself.

Thoughtfully, Uncle No'ccount wiped the harmonica on the seat of his trousers, ignoring the applause, and looked off into the distance. He could have taken an encore, but he didn't. I wondered when that battle had been lost and won.

Then the Cousins tumbled onstage, rowdy and rollicking, breaking the mood, but not quite setting up a mood of their own to replace it. Their routine leaned heavily on the 'We-uns is jes' plain folks' routine—in fact, they said it several times. The 'Jes' Plain Folks' attitude is the American equivalent of the British 'Working Class and Proud of it'. In both cases, it means that they expect you to despise them, so they're going to take the offensive by despising you first. It comes off better on the stage than face-to-face.

Things improved when the Cousins began to sing. Their voices were raucous, but adequate. They did better on instrumentals, but then, their orchestrations were very good. I wondered how much it had cost Sam and Nate.

Then it was Lou-Ann's turn. The way she stumbled across the stage and took her first pratfall *did* get a laugh. There was the sheet-lightning effect of flashbulbs off in the wings again—at least it would keep Maw Cooney happy, even if The Client went wild.

Helped too vigorously to her feet by Cousin Zeke, she fell off into the wings, then bounced back for another pratfall. The laughs kept coming, but she worked too hard for them, they cost too much. And she violated the cardinal rule of comedy: Never cross your eyes more than three times in any one minute.

The dialogue took a turn for the worse.

'I know a sad song, and a sad story to go with it. A sad, *true* story,' Lou-Ann said. 'Y'all wanna hear it, don't you?'

There was a frozen silence, then an embarrassed sprinkling of applause from the audience at thus being appealed to directly. Perhaps we're growing into a nation of voyeurs, thanks to films and television, but audiences prefer to think that they're invisible from the stage. It jars them to find that those strange characters acting out a charade for their amusement can actually see them, too. Nothing is more inconvenient than a one-way street when you find traffic coming the other way.

'There now, I jes' knew you were all my friends!' She spoiled the effect by turning and sticking her tongue out at the Cousins.

'Well, now, this here is a song written by a young fella back near the turn of the century. Him and his gal had been apart for a long while, but he was happy now because she was on a train comin' to marry him. An' while he was waitin' for the train to bring her to him, he wrote this song for her. But he didn't know that she was never goin' to hear it, 'cause even while he was writing it, the train had crashed and his sweetheart lay dying in the wreckage . . .'

It was bathos, but the house had hushed. Lou-Ann threw back her head and began to sing in a clear, sweet voice.

In the background, Cousin Homer took the bandana from Uncle No'ccount's pocket, shook the teeth out of it and handed them back to Uncle No'ccount, and caricatured wiping his eyes on the bandana. The other Cousins began making those gestures toward Lou-Ann.

There was a nasty, low-throated rumble from the audience. The Cousins looked startled.

Then the spotlight blacked out for a moment, returning as a soft baby blue spot centred on Lou-Ann's head and shoulders. You were only vaguely aware of the Cousins in the background, going through their accustomed gestures of derision.

But the laughs had stopped coming, and it unnerved her. She kept singing, but her eyes shifted restlessly. It didn't matter to her that the audience had been laughing *at* her and not with her. What mattered to her was the laughter, and that was gone. She wilted without it. Luckily, that didn't do the song any harm. Without knowing it, she had accomplished something I'd be willing to bet she had never done before. She had the audience in the palm of her hand as she finished the number.

She looked bewildered as the full spotlight came back to her and the applause broke loose. She bobbed a curtsy, swiftly, awkwardly, still glancing around like a wild, frightened thing. Then she dashed offstage.

The amplifiers went on, the beat loud, solid, hypnotic, for Black Bart's entrance.

> *'Homesteader, Homesteader,*
>   *'Ridin' alone . . .'*

His face was black and thunderous as he strode on. She had killed his entrance, and he knew it. There could be only one sad and lonely principal in the act. She had stolen the mood and part of it had exited with her.

Once again, there'd be hell to pay when the public performance was over. No wonder she had wanted to stick to comedy.

CHAPTER V

BACKSTAGE, after the house had emptied, the atmosphere was about as I had expected. I pasted a bright smile on my lips, prepared to congratulate and then side-step any members of the Troupe I was unfortunate enough to trip over. I simply wanted to collect Penny and Gerry before they got caught in the crossfire and, incidentally, exchange a few words with Sam, if possible. By this time, I wasn't sure whether I really had anything to say to Sam or not. It was the challenge of the whole thing which had roused my sporting blood.

I might have known Penny and Gerry wouldn't have been where I left them. Gerry had a fine nose for trouble. Where else would he be, then, but in the star dressing-room, watching the fray with interest—and with Penny? I was surprised, however, to find Sam there, too. I had thought he possessed a finer sense of self-preservation.

Lou-Ann was on the carpet—almost literally. She was crouched beside Black Bart's chair. Another couple of inches and she would have been kneeling.

'Bart,' she pleaded, 'honest, Bart. I didn't tell them to. I didn't know what was going to happen until they did it. Bart—you ain't mad at *me*?'

Why should she be any different? It was easy to see that Black Bart was mad at everybody. He had a fine line in sulks, and this was the most impressive I had yet seen. The black scowl on his face, the rigid line of his lips, the way his arms were tightly folded across his chest—they were all effective, if reminiscent. He was every outlaw in every bad Western you had ever seen, brooding until sundown, when he was going to stalk down that empty dirt road and kill himself a lawman. It was just as well that Black Bart had no gun, and that the nearest Sheriff was 3,000 miles away.

'Please, Bart,' Lou-Ann said. 'Tell me you ain't mad at me.'

Black Bart looked over her head impassively. I had a momentary hope that he was never going to speak again.

'If you want to take it out on anybody, Bart—' Sam, too, was tight-lipped and white-faced—'take it out on me. I gave the order for the big spot to be killed and the baby blue to be used.' I'd never realized Sam had this insane death-wish. He'd never shown any signs of suicidal tendencies when I'd known him in the States. 'Furthermore, it's going to stay that way from now on. It's right for the act.'

That brought Black Bart to his feet, quivering with fury. Sam went whiter than white, but stood his ground.

'What did you say?' Bart demanded dangerously.

'You heard me.' Sam's voice was almost steady. 'I told you before that that number shouldn't be played for laughs. Now I've proved it. From here on in, she warbles it straight. And the devil with the laughs.'

'Maybe you still ain't got the picture,' Black Bart said softly, still dangerously. 'She's *here* for laughs.

Look at her—you think any man's gonna look at her and *not* laugh?'

Lou-Ann rose, with terrible eagerness. 'I *told* him, Bart. I said I didn't want to do anything that wasn't funny.'

'You want the song to stay in—' Bart ignored her, still glaring at Sam—'then *I'll* sing it. It goes better with my image, anyhow.'

'I don't know.' Maw Cooney seemed to be tired of living, too. She came forward slowly to face Bart. 'The audience liked it. 'Course, they always go crazy for Lou-Ann, but this was something special. They—' she lowered her voice into an awed, hushed tone—'they really *loved* her. Maybe we *ought* to keep it in like that.'

There was a slight scrabbling noise, like rats abandoning ship, as the Cousins edged back against the wall. Bart took it quite mildly, for him. 'You think so, huh? Who told you you could think? *I* built this act, what *I* say goes. Just remember—none of you would be nothing, if it wasn't for me.'

'I don't know about that.' Maw Cooney's jaw set in a stubborn line. '*You* just remember a few things, yourself. Lou-Ann was pretty famous before you ever came on the scene. So you needn't think you're the big shot who's done it all. I tell you, you wouldn't be where you are today if you'd had to play the Nashville Circuit all by your lonesome. An' that ain't all—'

'Maw, Maw.' Lou-Ann was tugging at her sleeve anxiously. Perhaps she really loved the old bat—the silver cord was a wonderful thing. At any rate, she seemed concerned to stop Maw Cooney's tirade before Black Bart reached out those big hands that were twitching at his side and knotted them around Maw Cooney's neck. 'Let it go, Maw. Just forget it.'

'I ain't gonna forget it.' But Maw Cooney let herself be pulled back a couple of steps. 'You're too easy-going, my girl, that's your trouble. I don't know where you'd be, if you didn't have me to look out for your interests.'

'Better off.' But I was the only one to hear Sam's low murmur. Black Bart, head turning restlessly from side to side, had spotted a new vent for his anger. Uncle No'ccount and Crystal were trying to slip out of the door before he got around to raging at the rest of them. They didn't quite make it.

'You come back here,' he yelled. 'Where in hell do you think you're sneaking off to?'

'Nowhere, Bart.' Crystal halted in the doorway, hovering there. 'Just thought we'd like a little breath of fresh air, that's all.'

'There's plenty of air right here. Get back and sit down.' He glared at her while she came back into the room. Nasty grins broke out like a rash across the faces of the Cousins.

Uncle No'ccount still hovered in the doorway. 'I oughta go get some work done,' he said. 'You don't want *me*, do you, Bart?'

'Hell, I don't *want* none of you,' Bart snarled. 'But I'm stuck with you.' He swung back suddenly and caught up his big sombrero from the back of the chair, then grabbed Crystal by the wrist and thrust her towards the door.

'Okay,' he said, 'I'll give you some fresh air. Come on, we'll walk back to the hotel.'

There seemed to be a lot more air for the rest of us, and a lot fresher, too, once Bart had left the room. The

Cousins gave it a count of ten, then slithered out of the door themselves. That improved the atmosphere, too.

Sam crossed over to Lou-Ann and Maw Cooney, speaking to them in a rapid undertone I could not hear. Not that I was interested.

By that time, I had met Gerry's accusing eye. 'You should have told me,' he said reproachfully. 'You've let me go on living in a fool's paradise, when I should have been crawling on my hands and knees to the hyphenated-hag and trying to get back into her good graces—at least long enough to get us paid.'

'I don't know,' Penny said thoughtfully. 'He was super out on the stage, wasn't he? Maybe he's just tired after the performance. I'll bet he's awfully high-strung.'

'Child, child.' Gerry patted her head gently. 'Keep your youthful illusions, but don't let them run away with you. If ever I saw a prize candidate to join the Great Unmentionables at an early date—'

'Did you get some shots?' It was an unnecessary question, I just threw it in to cheer him up.

'I got some magnificent shots. Far better than any of them deserve.' He glanced across the room thoughtfully. 'You know, that girl has a wonderful bone structure. Why doesn't she try to look like a member of the human race?'

I knew what he meant. None of Gerry's birds would have been caught dead in last year's Quant, last season's restaurant, or last month's hairstyle. Lou-Ann, on the other hand, would have died before abandoning her 'comedy costume'. Somewhere, there must be a happy medium.

'. . . I don't care.' Maw Cooney's voice rose abruptly. 'He ain't been treating my Lou-Ann right for a long time now. I'm gonna go after him and give him a real good piece of my mind!'

'Maw!—' Lou-Ann caught at her elbow as she tried to leave. 'Just cool off, Maw. It's all right, honest—'

'There ain't nothing right about it! He should remember your position. He thinks he's the Great I-Am, and nobody else counts for nothing. Well, it's high time he learned different, and I'm gonna—'

'Okay, okay, but not just now, huh? We need you here.' Sam glanced over at me, signalling desperately. I was interested to find that he *could* remember I existed—when he needed me. 'Doug, bring the photographer over her, will you, please? We want to get some good shots of Lou-Ann, while we've got a clear field.'

Nothing else could have brought Maw Cooney to heel so quickly. 'Oh, well now, that's a real good idea,' she said, all the fire dying away. 'It sure is nice to know we've got a Road Manager who knows his onions.'

Sam winced. 'Thanks.' He turned to Lou-Ann briskly. 'Now, we'll just get rid of that—' He yanked off the appalling hat.

'No, give that back!' Lou-Ann clutched for it.

'Take it easy. We just want a couple of straight shots,' Sam held the hat out of reach. 'Be a good girl and get into your street clothes, will you?'

He should have known better. In the short time I had had to observe her, even I had realized that the one thing calculated to throw her into a blind panic was any suggestion that she come out from behind the mask of comedy and look or act like a normal human being.

She fought like a wildcat, or whatever the local fauna was in the territory she came from. Sam tossed the hat away and used both hands to defend himself. He wasn't doing too well. Maw Cooney circled them like a stray bitch, watching her chance to get in there and sink her teeth where they'd do the most damage.

The best idea I could come up with was to throw a bucket of cold water over them, but there was no water in the room. Only a half-empty bottle of bourbon, and I couldn't bring myself to waste it.

Gerry stopped them. The flash of light from the camera halted them. They blinked, and separated, dazed. Then Gerry stepped into the breach. He gave Lou-Ann his warmest smile. I had seen Gerry in action before. I could never copy his technique—I still didn't believe it. But it worked every time.

They have laws to protect poor fish. Dynamiting trout is illegal in all civilized countries. When civilization reaches a more advanced stage, they may get around to protecting people from onslaughts of sheer concentrated charm. (Or perhaps television will eventually prove an immunizing agent.)

Meanwhile, there is no defence. I watched Lou-Ann smooth her hair, pull down her jacket, and generally prove that a rag, a bone, and a hank of hair has the same reactions, no matter where in the world it originated. She gave Gerry a shy, hesitant smile.

'I got some splendid shots during the performance,' he told her. 'But now I'd like a few relaxed, natural pictures, for my own scrapbook—if nothing else.'

Lou-Ann still looked doubtful, but Maw Cooney dealt herself into the action at this stage.

'It can't do any harm,' she advised Lou-Ann. 'You jes' let the nice gentleman take any pictures he wants. After all—' she simpered at Gerry, who didn't turn a hair—'even if he takes them, that ain't to say he's going to pass them around, is it?'

'Assuredly not.' Gerry nearly bowed. 'I shouldn't dream of doing anything that didn't have your full approval.'

He had Lou-Ann's plaits piled coronet-style on top of her head by that time, and her jacket off. 'Suppose we just try this,' he murmured. He turned the jacket back to front and swathed her in it, hiding the awful blouse.

Sam watched him with narrowed eyes. Maw Cooney's eyes were narrow, too, but I thought I recognized the look in them. I had seen it before, in other hopeful mothers mentally measuring Gerry for a wedding-ring. That was always before they knew him very well.

CHAPTER VI

IF YOUR LUCK is in, you stand a good chance with an Award Presentation. Provided that no one declares war, assaults a photogenic female, or ingeniously murders a spouse, there's a sporting chance that some desperate editor will throw you into an empty space.

It took no effort at all, next day, to persuade Penny to gather a few friends into a Black Bart Fan Club and elect her President. Since Sam was ultimately footing the bill, we decided on a silver-plated miniature guitar—but big enough to photograph well—and I sent Penny off to find one and get it engraved.

I was on the phone, putting out the photo call, when Sam walked into the office. He sat down and breathed heavily for a few minutes.

'Can't you afford a building with an elevator?' he finally wheezed.

'You mean a lift,' I told him. 'Since you ask, we can't. Apart from which, it's considered healthier for people to take gentle exercise—like climbing a few stairs or going for long walks every day. I thought your doctors over there were dead keen on the idea.'

'Then let them climb the stairs!' Sam was recovering enough to sit up and take notice. He looked round the room carefully, obviously deciding that Nathan's investment hadn't been frittered away in pursuit of sybaritic luxury. The furniture was second-hand Utility, and even at the rate bygones were coming back into style these days, we weren't going to live long enough to see any of it make us a profit on the antique market.

'Would you like a cup of tea? Or a cigar?' It wasn't much, but it was the best I could offer. He shot me an odd glance and shook his head.

Well, I'd done my best to be hospitable. I settled back and waited for him to make the next move. After all this time, I could hardly believe he had come here of his own free will. I still half expected him to vanish in a puff of smoke.

'Nice little place you've got here,' he lied half-heartedly.

'It isn't much, but it's home.'

He nodded glumly, still glancing around the room. Perhaps he'd had orders from Nate to come and inspect the place, but he looked more like a nervous man trying to spot the Fire Exit in case of an emergency. If there was a point to his visit, it didn't seem that he was going to let me in on it.

'Sure you wouldn't like a cup of tea?' I pressed.

He shook his head again, and that was the last indication I had from him that he was aware of my presence in the room. After that, he just slumped in the chair, staring into space.

'Try a cigar—they're improving with age.' I used it as an excuse to lean across the desk, holding the box out to him, so that I could look at his eyes. The pupils appeared to be normal. I hadn't really thought he was on drugs, but you never can be too sure these days.

But no, the trouble wasn't drugs. The trouble might just possibly be Trouble. Sam, the more I studied him, looked like a man with the Giant Economy-Size package of Trouble on his shelf.

He was still ignoring me, so I gave it up for a bad job and went back to telephoning. I sent out half a dozen more photo calls to newspapers and agencies before I looked up again to find him staring at me.

This time he knew I was there. And he seemed to wish I wasn't. Well, that was easy enough to remedy— all he had to do was get up and go away. It was *my* office, after all.

'What's this about Fan Club kids?' he demanded.

'You heard the call I was putting out. The Black Bart Fan Club of London will present Bart with a silver guitar tomorrow at 2.00 p.m., in honour of his first English tour.'

'These kids—' there was a peculiar urgency in his manner—'how kiddish are they?'

I saw his point. I wouldn't like a bunch of impressionable kids to trip over Black Bart in one of his black moods. 'Relax,' I said, 'they're all in on it. My secretary is the President—she'll be presenting the Award. It *would* be nice, though, if you could keep the Great Man civil for the occasion. For the sake of the Press, of course.'

'Oh, he'll be okay.' Sam did relax. He slumped again, but managed not to go back into his former trance. I felt we were making progress. It emboldened me to ask a direct question.

'What the hell is going on, Sam? What the bloody hell is *really* going on with your bunch?'

He leaped a mile, then pulled himself together. He

even managed a smile, but his eyes had resumed their restless inventory of the room. 'I don't know what you mean,' he said doggedly.

'Cut it out, Sam. You're not that dumb—and neither am I.'

'Okay, Doug.' He faced me squarely. 'I'll be honest with you.'

Automatically, I braced myself for a lie.

'We've had our little problems. I mean, it's not just one big happy family—the way the act plays. Most of them aren't even related—you can't expect it. But they're good boys and girls, they'll settle down. They're a little out of their depth, being in a foreign country, too.' He laughed falsely. 'To tell you the truth, so am I. That's why I'm so glad we've got you, Douggie boy, we're depending on you to see us through.'

Well, I could see through him. Perhaps that was a start. 'Try it again,' I said. 'I'm not buying that one. It's hollow when you thump it.'

That laugh of his was beginning to grate on my nerves. 'Ah, you're too clever for us, Douggie boy. I'll admit there are wheels within wheels. It's an awkward situation.'

'Then you'd better fill me in on it. You know it's as important for a public relations man to know what to avoid as it is to know what to publicize.'

'Well.' He clawed blindly for a cigarette, avoiding my eyes. 'It's like this.' He paused to light the cigarette, and I lost him again. He stared abstractedly at the match until it burned down almost to his fingers, then he shook it out and took to staring at the lighted tip of the cigarette instead.

'Come along,' I prodded him, 'you can tell *me*. I'm

on *your* side, you know. I don't care if Uncle No'ccount runs an illegal still in his backyard down yonder—I'm not going to shop him to the Revenue men.'

'Naw.' Sam shook his head impatiently. 'Nothing like that. There's nothing wrong with Uncle No'ccount— he's clean as a whistle.'

'And what's buzzing with the Cousins?'

'You heard about Ezra?' Sam twitched nervously. 'That was nothing, really—just kid stuff. Playing around with love potions. It could have happened to anyone.'

'Not in *my* circles,' I said firmly.

'Yeah, well, not in mine, either. But things are different way down South. So, when he got this wild passion for an older woman four or five years ago, he put some Spanish fly in her drink.'

'My God! Isn't that stuff poison?'

'Yeah, he found that out. He'd given her an overdose, too, to make matters worse. He was lucky she pulled through.'

'The only reason the jury let him off, I presume.'

'Hell, it didn't get *that* far. I told you she was an older woman—friend of his mother's, in fact. She didn't press charges. Soon as she was feeling better, she couldn't help seeing the funny side of it.'

'All good clean fun,' I said weakly.

'That's right. And it sure taught Ezra a lesson. We won't have any trouble with *him*. And the rest of the Cousins are A-Okay.'

'Good. That helps narrow the field, doesn't it?' I had a fairly shrewd idea to whom the field was going to narrow down, but felt I ought not to rush Sam too much. He'd tell me, now that he'd started. It might take a while, but I hadn't any plans for the afternoon.

'I mean, you've got to understand the background to this set-up before you can know how awkward it really is.'

'Okay, fill me in.'

'Sure, I'm going to.' Again he gave the imitation of a man wishing someone would yell 'Fire' so that he could beat a fast, explicable retreat. No one obliged.

'You see, it's like this.' He gave up with a sigh. 'They—the Big Boys in New York—have kept their eyes on the Nashville Scene for a long while now. Some really big ones have come out of there since the days of Hank Williams. They may start out as Hillbilly, or Country and Western, but they can be turned into Folk—and that means International appeal today. The Madison Avenue boys keep an eye out for stars they can build, characters with staying power, who can capture the public and keep them. Preferably, ones who won't go off the rails with a bit of success and start blowing their brains out with LSD, or drinking a couple of quarts of corn squeezings and then racing their sports car down a highway playing "chicken" with oil tankers.'

'And so, with all those sterling qualifications in mind, they picked on Black Bart?' I said incredulously.

'Well, uh, no,' Sam said. 'As a matter of fact, they picked on Lou-Ann.'

'Lou-Ann?' That was even harder to believe. 'You can't seriously mean you think that that little—'

'Cool it!' Sam held up his hand, eyes narrowed dangerously. 'Just think it over for a minute. There's always a shortage of good female comics.'

'*Good* is the word.' But I didn't say it too loudly. Something about Sam's attitude was beginning to proclaim 'vested interest', even to my uncritical eyes.

'Good,' he repeated, on firmer ground. 'These things

go in cycles. We feel the public may be tired of pretty girls standing up and snarling protest songs at them. There's room for a comedienne who can also sing ballads and tearjerkers. There hasn't been one since Judy Canova—and look how big *she* was.'

'I remember,' I said, treading cautiously. 'But I don't think Lou-Ann is quite—'

'And look at Dorothy Shay—the Park Avenue Hillbilly,' Sam went on enthusiastically. 'You get some fast patter and some sophisticated material and—'

'Now, I *know* Lou-Ann isn't Park Avenue Hillbilly material,' I said firmly. 'Hillbilly, yes. Park Avenue, no.'

'Okay, so the kid needs a little more polish, a little more class. But then, there's nowhere she can't go—' He broke off. Nothing I had said had been able to get through to him, but now something from the back of his own mind stopped him. He deflated like a punctured tyre.

'Nowhere she couldn't have gone,' he corrected.

Here it came. He slumped in his chair, staring into space, his head turning from side to side in agonizing, unbelieving negation.

'Then the whole thing blew up,' he said. 'Right in our faces. After we had their names on the contract, but before we had time to start the star build-up.'

'Bart?' I asked.

'Bart,' he agreed grimly. 'We'd been planning to phase him out of the act. You know the routine. A little less to do every few shows, then part of the background, then—pfft. He quietly disappears. And, all the while, Lou-Ann would have been coming to the fore, getting known, taking over the show.'

'But it didn't work out that way.'

'He got hold of the 'Homesteader' song. They cut the

disc. Nobody realized it was going to be that big a hit. Now, he's dead centre in the Public Eye, and we're stuck with him.' Sam got to his feet wearily, as though the effort of finally telling me the story had drained his last reserves of strength.

'Did Bart know what you'd planned?'

'Hell, no. We were keeping it Top Secret—Agency level only.' Sam began moving towards the door slowly. 'You want to know something funny?' He bared his teeth in a brief, mirthless grimace.

'Now, Bart wants us to get rid of Lou-Ann. Phase *her* out of the act, and just leave him and the boys. More appeal to the public, he says. His female fans.'

'Well, why not?' I couldn't see why Sam was making such a grand tragedy production of it. 'It seems like the perfect answer. You just split up the act. And then you have *two* star acts. Perhaps even, two big television shows.' I should have known that, if the answer were that easy, Sam would have thought of it.

'It doesn't quite work that way.' He paused at the door and turned back to me. 'Nothing in life is ever that simple. You see, Lou-Ann is married to him. Not only that, but she's still so crazy, out-of-her-skull nuts about the bastard that what he says goes!'

I spent the rest of the afternoon in a fool's paradise, thinking that Sam had finally confided in me. I knew the worst—and it had nothing to do with Perkins & Tate. It was the Agency's problem.

After cleaning up a few jobs for remaining clients, and finishing the photo call, I went over and opened the window, and leaning against the window frame, looked down at the Thames. I even had one of our left-over cigars, while the band music from the Embankment Gardens floated up to me, inducing that curiously inspiring euphoria music from a brass band always does—you feel that a world which produced Gilbert and Sullivan and John Philip Sousa can't be all bad.

It had also produced Black Bart, but I still felt inclined to forgive it that—any world can have an off day. Besides, Black Bart and the Troupe would soon step back on board ship and return to the States, leaving Perkins & Tate (Public Relations) Ltd solvent and with a new lease of life.

And, given just a little more time, I had no doubt that the Agency would manage to split Black Bart and Lou-Ann into two equally successful acts, despite Sam's pessimism.

Perhaps a nice quiet divorce all round—professionally and personally. Lou-Ann might be crazy about Bart, but he certainly didn't show any signs of affection for her. *And* she was sharing a room with her mother. (Which brought up another thought—did Maw know? Or was it part of the problem that it was a secret marriage?) If Lou-Ann was reluctant to leave Bart, perhaps it was because the idea hadn't been put to her in the right way. The way he was ferrying Crystal around with him ought to provide evidence in any court in any country . . .

The telephone rang just then, and I eyed it mistrustfully. It had been a long time since incoming calls were good news. They still weren't.

'I want to talk to Mr Perkins.' The sharp voice twanged at my eardrums.

'Yes,' I said. She misunderstood.

'You put me right through to your boss—immediately—

and don't be so sassy! I'll have you know my daughter is an important client.'

It was no time to argue. I tapped the receiver on the desk a couple of times, ran a pencil around the dial, snapped my fingers into the mouthpiece, then cleared my throat and tried again.

'Good afternoon. Douglas Perkins here.'

'About time, too. You ought to train that office boy of yours to answer the phone better. He was downright rude to me.'

'I'm terribly sorry, Mrs Cooney. I'll speak to him severely.'

'I should hope so. I don't mind for myself, but as the mother of Lou-Ann Mars, I ought to be accorded decent treatment. And you ought to be careful for yourself, too, he could insult important people some day. You know, you've got to have an efficient staff, if you want to get ahead in the world. Talent can do a lot, but you need good backing. Believe me, I know.'

It was then that I had my bright idea. At least, like most catastrophic conceptions, it seemed a good idea at the time.

'I'm glad you rang, Mrs Cooney. I was going to call you and suggest dinner this evening, if you're not engaged.'

'Dinner?' She sounded so suspicious that, for a moment, I wondered if it had turned into one of those double-meaning slang words that lurk like traps in the undergrowth of Anglo-American relations. 'I'm sorry, I'm afraid Lou-Ann is eating with Mr Marcowitz tonight. They've just left. Maybe we could make it tomorrow night?'

'If you'd rather. But *you're* the one I asked.'

'Me?' I couldn't blame her for being incredulous. I would have been myself, had someone told me earlier that I would issue this invitation. 'But I only called up to find out if those pictures your friend took of Lou-Ann are ready yet. I wanted a couple of nice ones to send back to the fan magazines for the next *See the Stars with Lou-Ann Mars* column.'

'The film is being processed at the laboratory now. We should have a set of contact prints tomorrow. Meanwhile, I'll come round for you in about an hour, shall I?'

The Italian restaurant was close enough to Soho for one to stretch a point, providing that one were dealing with American tourists. I'd taken the precaution of telephoning first and warning them that I was bringing along an American journalist—well, the column *was* in six fan magazines.

Luigi greeted us like minor royalty and bowed us to a table. We got the full red carpet treatment, with a personal consultation over the menu, and Maw Cooney was suitably impressed.

'My goodness,' she sighed, as he disappeared into the kitchen to supervise the chef, 'wasn't he nice? Why, he couldn't have been nicer if—if Lou-Ann was with us. I surely would like to tell folks about this. Do you suppose—' she looked around furtively—'do you suppose I could write all about this—him bowing and suchlike—in my column, and make out like Lou-Ann was with us, and it was on account of her he was being so nice?'

'I don't see why not,' I said. 'If you're worried about it not being quite . . . accurate, perhaps we could come back another time, and bring Lou-Ann with us.'

'So it would be true, after all!' She leaned back and

beamed at me. 'You are a gentleman. A true gentleman.' She scrabbled in her handbag and brought out a ballpoint pen and a tiny notebook. 'I just want to set a bit of it down, so's I don't forget it later. All that red velvet and crystal chandeliers—it's near as good as some of them real fancy places in New Orleans that used to be cathouses before the Vice Squad cleaned up the city. Folks sure will be interested to hear all about it.'

She seemed to be at her happiest talking, so I let her ramble on. There was a certain paucity of subject matter, but she was in the best mood I'd ever seen her in, so I concentrated on the food and made encouraging noises when she paused.

I had Lou-Ann's scintillating babyhood with the lasagne ('right from the minute she opened her baby-blue eyes, I knowed she was something special'); and Lou-Ann's meteoric rise to fame with the veal scallopini ('she won three amateur contests in a row before she was even in her teens, so I knowed I was right to be grooming her for stardom').

By the zabaglione, we had reached Lou-Ann's present state of theatrical acclaim, and the moment seemed to be right for me to put my idea into execution.

There used to be a song called 'If I Knew Then, What I Know Now', which was fairly popular when I was in the States. They should have had a full orchestra of sobbing violins playing it at that moment, instead of just Luigi whistling 'Santa Lucia' off-key in the kitchen.

'It's too bad things have turned out the way they have,' I said.

'Too bad?'

'With the "Homesteader" song being such a big success for Bart—just when the Agency wanted to ease him

out of the act and concentrate on building Lou-Ann.'
That was the great idea. Just drop the word to Maw
Cooney, and count on her doing the work of persuading
Lou-Ann to drop Bart.

'The Agency wanted to do that!' Hook, line and
sinker. She goggled at me—for a moment, I saw where
Lou-Ann had found that grotesque grimace of hers. Was
it unconscious, or did she realize that she was parody-
ing her mother? 'I never heard nothing about that.' Her
eyes narrowed thoughtfully. 'I never reckoned they had
that much good sense.'

'It was too early to tell anyone,' I said. 'Probably
they were afraid the word would get around if anyone
knew. It was to be a gradual easing-out. I think they
were afraid Bart would make trouble.'

'Let him try!' Her eyes were slits now, her fingers
flexed like claws. The lioness ready to do battle for her
cub. I was momentarily unnerved. What had I un-
leashed? 'I reckon two can play at trouble-making, and
I know enough to keep that there boy in his place.

'I'm sure everything will be all right,' I soothed. 'It
simply means that they'll have to delay their plans.
You'll just have to wait a bit longer.'

'We've waited long enough!' She glanced at me, then,
with conscious effort, she relaxed. 'I take it most kindly
of you to let me in on this little secret—and I know
Lou-Ann will appreciate it, too. But now, if you don't
mind I think I'd like to go back to the hotel. I've sure
got a lot of new thinking and planning to do.'

CHAPTER VII

THE HOTEL was near Fleet Street and the drinks were free, so a reasonable number of journalists showed up for the Presentation. We had about eight photographers, too. Most of them were from *Dairyman's Gazette* type of mags, but a few were from actual fan magazines, albeit tending towards the shoestring bi-monthly variety, which would probably fold before they could use the pictures. At least, it gave the Client the impression we were doing a good job for him.

Just in case nobody showed up, of course, I had Gerry festooned with flashbulbs and on stand-by. He entered too lavishly into the spirit of the occasion for my taste— with all those legitimate photographers around, he needn't have taken so many pictures. Those flashbulbs cost money.

Penny had dressed up in her abbreviated best to make the presentation, and looked even younger than her fifteen years. Which was fine, it was the kids we wanted to sell Black Bart to. Sam had made arrangements for a single of 'Homesteader' to be released at the end of the week.

Somehow, Penny had dragooned her three mates back into their school uniforms and kept their make-up to a minimum, so that they looked about thirteen—just the age when pocket-money is being stretched to buy records. They kept together and made a nice background for photos as Penny stepped forward to present the silver guitar to Black Bart.

Bart grinned at her, with more animation than I had ever seen him display before. I began to wonder if I had wronged him—he obviously had a soft spot for children, and wasn't going to be difficult over this presentation. If he liked animals, too, it must mean that he wasn't all bad. Unfortunately, he was bad enough.

He continued being more lamb than black sheep. He held the silver guitar on high, still grinning with delight at Penny. My first sense of unease came when I caught a glimpse of Sam over his shoulder.

Sam had gone a nasty greeny-white, and was dabbing at his brow with a handkerchief balled up in one hand, while gnawing at the remnants of fingernails on the other hand. There was an expression in his eyes I never wanted to see again. I was now certain that there was more to this whole deal than the cards Sam had turned face upwards so far. I began to feel rather greeny-white myself.

The Client seemed to feel that more was indicated than just a simple thank-you. With a quick movement, he caught Penny to him and kissed her. She wriggled back, but couldn't get away. Imprisoning her, with an arm around her shoulders, he grinned at the cameras.

'Ain't she just as pretty as a waterhole on a hot day to a thirsty man?' he inquired. 'Honey, you're so cute, I tell you what I'm a-gonna do—just for you . . . and your cute little old friends,' he added as an afterthought. 'I'm gonna sing our song just especially for you. Sort of a Command Performance. Now, how do you like that?'

Penny smiled dutifully and tried to slip away to join her friends, who were standing an enviable five paces away, but Bart didn't let go. He gave the downbeat to the Cousins, with his free hand and, looking deep into Penny's eyes, began to sing.

'*Homesteader, Homesteader,*
  '*Ridin' alone . . .*'

There is nothing worse than being sung at. If you look away, you're afraid of seeming discourteous and possibly putting the singer off stroke; whereas, if you look back into those searching eyes, you're afraid of giving the impression that you return whatever dubious sentiments are being yodelled at you. And singers always feel that they're doing you such a big favour by singing to you. I once had a girl-friend who was a music student and, to my dying day, will remember the exhibition she made of me by choosing to serenade me—complete with a meaningful gaze into my eyes—on a crowded escalator at Piccadilly Circus tube station. She never was able to figure out what ended the romance so abruptly, but it was the expressions on the faces of those gliding past us on the downward side of the escalator. Horrified to a man, and amused to a woman, they seemed to be saying, 'Good lord, can't the chap control that girl—and in public too!'

As for me then, so for Penny now, there was no escape. The Perkins & Tate funds wouldn't run to a rise in salary, but I determined to give her a bonus and get it back on the Client's bill later. This was above and beyond the call of duty.

The flashbulbs continued popping all the way through

the song, but Penny was a nice sensible girl and kept a
determined smile fixed on her face. I could see from
her eyes, though, that she had just resigned from the
Black Bart Fan Club. As I said, she was a nice sensible
girl.

Finishing the song, the Client squeezed Penny to him
again, but she turned her head at the last moment to
smile at the camera, so he had to, as well. Sam, unable
to get a purchase on any shreds of fingernails on either
hand now, had compromised by quietly beginning to
shred his handkerchief into tatters.

I moved forward to the rescue, and heard the Client
say, 'How's about you and me going out for a quiet
drink?'

'No, really,' Penny gasped. 'I have to go home and
do my homework.' As an attempt to discourage him by
reference to her youth, it was a failure. Black Bart
chuckled insinuatingly.

'Why don't you just go get your homework and bring
it back here, then? I jest love helping kiddies with their
homework. I got a real talent for it.'

At least he kept his voice low. The Press were leaving, and Penny's schoolmates too far away to hear. Sam
had been out of earshot, too, but he charged forward
nervously, as though he knew what was going on. I
decided it was time to speak to Sam again.

'Come on, Bart.' Sam pulled him away from Penny.
'It's time to start for the theatre. You want to check
those lighting cues again, and I don't think the amplifier
sounded so good at last night's performance. We ought
to—'

'Leave me alone!' Bart shrugged Sam off. 'Leave *us*

alone.' He started for Penny again, but I stepped in front of him.

'We'd like a few more pictures of you, Bart,' I said. 'You and the Cousins—with Lou-Ann.' I signalled Gerry forward with the camera.

Bart hesitated and, while he was unsure, I nudged him farther away from Penny. She wasted no time in quietly heading for the exit, leaving her friends to trail after her. Bart put out his hand, as though to try to stop her, but the Cousins and Lou-Ann closed in on us and the moment of danger was past.

'You damned fool,' Sam snarled softly at me. 'I thought you said you were having your secretary present the award. What the hell went wrong?'

'Nothing,' I said. 'Penny *is* my secretary.'

'Why, you dawg!' The Client whirled on me, giving me a conspiratorial slap on the back. 'They's more to you than I suspected. Who'd'a' thought it?' He guffawed loudly.

'Just get over there and pose.' Sam shoved him into the corner. 'And shut up!'

Still snuffling with laughter, Black Bart let himself be angled into position while Gerry took half a dozen shots. Sam supervised the session, then dismissed the Troupe and turned to Gerry and me.

'Come upstairs!' The velvet gloves were off, and the whiplash of command was in his voice. Little Brother was exercising his authority—with a sudden vengeance. 'Both of you. I want to talk to you.'

Sam slammed the door of his room on us as soon as we were inside and whirled on us. On me. 'Are you crazy?' he demanded. 'What the hell do you mean, dragging a kid like that near Bart? Are you *trying* to start trouble?'

'What does he mean, "a kid like that"?' Gerry caught the air of belligerency. 'What's the matter with Penny? She's a nice kid.'

'I think that's what he means.' A lot of things were beginning to come clear, and I didn't like the shape of any of them. 'Sam, suppose you put us in the picture. All the way in.'

'Have a drink.' It was surrender. He was in no position to keep up the boss routine. Sam brought out a bottle of bourbon and poured stiff ones. He didn't bother with water in his.

'What's this all about?' Gerry dumped the camera equipment on the bed and accepted his drink with suspicion.

'How old is that Penny kid?' Sam asked.

'Fifteen.'

'Jesus!' He shuddered and gulped at his bourbon. It did nothing to alleviate the greenish tinge which was creeping back into his face. 'How soon do they throw them into the labour market over here, anyway?'

'School leaving age is fifteen. Penny is going to business college and working part-time for us. As you've probably gathered, the business isn't flourishing quite well enough to run a full-time secretary.'

Sam shook his head, and waved away the reference to balance sheets. They were the least of his worries at the moment. 'Jesus!' he said again.

'Sam,' I said, 'tell us.'

He tried his favourite trick of gazing into space, but there was no escape there any longer. His eyes wavered and met mine with a sick expression. But it was time to be relentless.

'Bart,' I prodded. 'You've had trouble with him before?'

Sam nodded weakly.

'Perhaps that's the real reason for this unscheduled English tour, with no advance publicity?'

Sam nodded again.

'Obviously, you two know what you're talking about,' Gerry said plaintively, 'but do you think you could let me in on this meeting of minds?'

'I think the Client likes little girls,' I said. 'Too much.'

'What do you mean?' Gerry wasn't usually so obtuse, but I couldn't blame his mind for boggling.

'Jailbait!' Sam turned on him. 'Lolitas. San Quentin Quail. Under-age,' he spelled it out, 'so that, even if they say they consented, it's still statutory rape.'

'In short,' I repeated, 'the Client is a child molester. Female children.'

Gerry reeled, but rallied. 'How very different,' he murmured weakly, 'from the home life of our own dear queans.'

'And the real reason for this sudden urge for Olde Worlde culture?'

'He got away from us on that New England tour.' Sam was a defeated man. 'Hell, we couldn't chain him up. And that stupid lug couldn't get it into his head that there was a difference between the daughter of a New England doctor and the daughter of some Southern sharecropper. Instead of Big Daddy striding round with the horsewhip, ready to be bought off, the Yankee yelled for the law. The Agency is doing its best to come to some settlement, but I've orders to keep Bart over here until they succeed in quashing the indictment.'

'No wonder they decided Lou-Ann was a better bet for stardom.' I was feeling a bit sick. 'Or is there something wrong with her, too?'

'What the hell do you mean by that?' That brought Sam to his feet fighting.

'Well, she *is* sharing a room with her mother, instead of her ever-loving spouse.'

'That's not her fault. It's all because of that goddamned bitch, anyway. She hasn't shared a room with Bart since they got married.'

'I can see it was a real love-match. Was that when Crystal moved in?'

'Crystal—are you crazy?' Sam sat down again and reached for his drink. 'Crystal is Bart's sister, that's all. I meant Maw Cooney. It's all her fault.'

'I can understand her not approving.'

'Approving? You think Maw Cooney didn't approve?' Sam laughed harshly. 'Let me tell you, she engineered the whole thing. Lou-Ann was only fourteen at the time. She as good as pushed her into bed with Bart and, in the morning, dear old Maw was standing by the pillow with a shotgun—and a Justice of the Peace.'

It explained a lot of things, but not quite the hold Maw Cooney seemed to have over Bart. 'Why?' I asked. 'Bart must have dodged a lot of shotgun weddings in his time. How come he let Maw Cooney force him up the aisle?'

'Because she had the biggest, blackest shotgun of all—and both barrels were loaded. With more than buckshot.' Sam refilled his bourbon and passed the bot-

tle around. 'You see, in the . . . heat of the moment
. . . Bart didn't notice that he was driving along a very
winding road. The motel they ended up at was across
the State Line. That made it a violation of the Mann
Act—transporting a female across the State Lines for
immoral purposes. That took it out of the realm of
quaint little local laws and turned it into a Federal of-
fence. Maw Cooney had him by the short hairs, because if she yelled Cop, he faced a term in the Federal
Penitentiary.'

'So he did the decent thing and made an honest
woman out of the little gal.' All the cards were face up
now, and I was right—I'd been dealt a full hand of
jokers.

'Since when,' Sam drained his glass, 'he has ignored
the blushing bride. As the man says, you can lead a
horse to water . . .'

'You know,' Gerry said thoughtfully, 'I've never re-
gretted it more that we don't have a drinks firm among
our clients. This seems a night when there's nothing for
it but to get drunk. It won't do any good, but it will
certainly make me feel better.'

'There's another bottle of bourbon.' Sam squinted at
it thoughtfully. 'Be my guests.'

Before I did, I wanted to be certain of just one more
point. 'That's the *full* story? We know the absolute worst
now? You don't have a couple more cards up your
sleeve—like a brace of Aces of Spades?'

'Scout's honour.' Sam raised his hand. 'Believe me,
if there was anything more, *I* couldn't stand it. Not even
to help Nathan out.'

I glanced at Gerry and he nodded. We believed Sam.

There was nothing worse up his sleeve, but he had already dealt us enough.

I poured more bourbon, knowing, even as I did so, that it was not going to help me to relax.

By late the next morning, the insistent pounding in my head had slackened off and the situation looked better. At least, so far as the Perkins & Tate end of it was concerned. For our sins, Gerry and I had once handled an ageing Broadway star during his English tour, and the experience we had gathered trying to keep him from his craving, and sober enough to go onstage every night ought to stand us in good stead watching over Black Bart. It should be easier to spot Bart sneaking off the rails, since his penchant didn't come in half, quarter and miniature sizes, and couldn't be tucked away into convenient desk drawers or coat pockets.

All we had to do, then, was keep Bart away from the under-age segment of his public. Autograph books could be collected at the Stage Door and brought to Bart to sign in his dressing-room, so there would be no gathering of kids for him to plough through after the performance. Sam could continue to dog Bart's footsteps whenever he stepped outside the hotel and, even though it would cut into what we laughingly referred to as 'our other business', Gerry and I could take turns on guard duty when Sam wanted time off. Oh yes, and it might be a good idea to make sure that Bart never came near the office or got within sighting distance of Penny again.

Having decided that, I thought I'd covered all contingencies. I even thought it didn't sound too difficult. A strenuous programme, perhaps, but not an impossible one. But then, I was a hundred years younger in those days.

For one thing, I had forgotten the rest of the Troupe. I realized this when the telephone rang, and I heard the plaintive whine at the other end of the line.

'Douglas, I'm right disappointed in you. I do think you ought to see to it that Lou-Ann gets some kind of Award now, with pictures, and all. Her Public expects it.'

My head began throbbing again. 'Good morning, Mrs Cooney. How are you today?'

'Like I said, I'm disappointed. I did think you was a friend of ours.'

'I was,' I said. 'I am. I'm sorry you're disappointed, Mrs Cooney. But, you know, Bart *does* have the Top of the Charts hit, so it's Bart we must concentrate on. I *did* get Lou-Ann into some of the pictures, however.'

'Yes, I know. I understand your position—' her voice dropped meaningfully—'like you explained it so good to me the other night. But you got to think of Lou-Ann's position, too, and her future. That Bart—he's nothing but a flash in the pan. And I know how come he got that song to sing, too—it shoulda gone to Lou-Ann— but we won't bother about that right now. Don't you worry, though, I'm gonna see that something like that don't never happen again.'

I immediately began to worry. 'Mrs Cooney, I hope you won't mention anything I told you the other night. It was in strictest confidence, and for your information only—'

'That's right,' she interrupted firmly. 'And that's just why I'm calling you now. Because I know you got Lou-

Ann's interests at heart—even if it don't always seem
like it.'

'Mrs Cooney, I assure you—'

'Now, I want to get together with you for a nice long
talk about what we can do to promote Lou-Ann over
here. I already got some good ideas. I think you ought
to get Lou-Ann to open some of them village fêtes like
you read about in English novels. You might not realize
it, but Lou-Ann is no stranger to that kind of thing.
She's real good at it. Why, she opened the State Agri-
cultural Fair and the County Stock Show at home last
year, and they gave her an honorary bronze medal for
hog-calling. I mean, that little girl is just loaded with
talent. She'd liven up any of your old fêtes good and
proper.'

'I'm terribly sorry, Mrs Cooney,' I said, 'but my other
phone is ringing. I do agree that we must talk together
soon. Perhaps next week. You've certainly given me a
great deal to think about.'

I rang off quickly, before she could say anything
more, and staggered off in search of an aspirin.

But when a day starts like that, it usually goes on like
that. Penny's mother telephoned to report that Penny
had 'caught a chill' and wouldn't be in for the rest of
the week. I didn't blame her. I told her mother that we
were sorry to hear that, and that we'd see that Penny
got her salary just the same. We'd collect it from the
Client somewhere among the other fees.

I know that the human race would be in a bad way
without mothers, but I'd had enough of them for one
day, so I decided to clear out of the office before any
more could call.

I remembered the card in my pocket from one of our

PR friends—an invitation to an early afternoon film show in Leicester Square to demonstrate a new colour process, with an urgent 'Come and help swell the ranks' scrawled across the accompanying compliments slip. I could roam in there, looking like an interested advertising man, and try to catnap while the last of my hangover twinged itself out.

There turned out, as usual, to be more swelling than ranks at the showing. Afterwards, some of the crowd gathered round to congratulate me on the new Perkins & Tate account. It sounded good, handling Black Bart, and I didn't disillusion them. We went out for a few drinks at a new restaurant someone else was opening, and made a meal of the canapés. It was all very convivial.

During the course of the evening, nothing succeeding like success—or the appearance of it—I was sounded out by a couple of colleagues on accounts they didn't feel able to handle. 'Show biz, old boy, rather out of my line, but you—' Even with the spectre of Black Bart at my elbow, I didn't quail. Just signified enough interest to be approachable at a future time, but not enough to seem anxious for the work. Nor did I enquire too closely as to why they were being so generous with promising accounts. It was a lovely evening, I was off duty for the moment, and it was no time to go counting the teeth of gift horses.

I relaxed and enjoyed it. Which was just as well. It was the last peaceful evening I had.

CHAPTER VIII

THE TELEPHONE woke me in the morning. I stumbled
out into the office and snatched up the receiver, trying
to sound bright and alert, just in case it wasn't as early
as my numb brain insisted it was. 'Perkins & Tate. Good
morning.'

'This you, Jean?' a voice twanged in my ear.

'Sorry, wrong number. There's no Jean here.' On
second thought, perhaps there was. But I had no intention of barging into Gerry's bedroom to find out. In any
case, presumably she wouldn't want to be receiving calls
from a male voice.

'No—wait, don't hang up. I said this is Eugene. Eugene Hatfield.' It didn't leave me any more enlightened.

'I beg your pardon?'

There was a deep, depressed sigh. 'Uncle No'ccount,
I guess I'd better say.'

'I'm sorry.' I was. I don't know why it hadn't occurred to me that he must have had a real name. People
aren't born and christened Uncle No'ccount. Something
in that sigh had spoken of a long erosion of identity,
and I felt a little more had slipped away through my
carelessness. 'I just got up—I'm not fully awake yet.'

'That's all right,' he said glumly. 'I'm sorry I woke

you, but I guess you'd better get over here right away. There's all hell breaking loose. That's what I called to tell you. Sam can't come to the phone. He's too busy.'

'Why? What's happened?'

'Seems like Maw Cooney never came home last night. Lou-Ann is worried out of her mind.'

'But that's silly. The woman is over twenty-one. Perhaps she just—' But it would be a brave man who dared. I began to see why Lou-Ann was so worried.

'Believe me, she ain't the type. Even if she was, she'd have called and made some excuse so's Lou-Ann didn't worry. It might upset her performance. Maw'd never want that.'

And that was true enough. I didn't like it. True, there wasn't much I *did* like about the Troupe. But this I liked even less.

'I'll get dressed,' I said, 'and be over there as soon as I can.'

'We're all at Bart's place,' Uncle No'ccount said. 'Tryin' to think of something encouraging to say. Lou-Ann's cutting up pretty bad.' With that cheery bulletin, he rang off.

I *did* check to see if Gerry was in his bedroom then, but there was no sign of his having been there recently. Off nesting with one of his birds, I presumed. Which was no help to me, as usual. I went back to my own room and dressed quickly.

The Cousins were leaving as I arrived. They sidled past me with the eager escaping faces of males who had been subjected to an overdose of female hysterics.

Lou-Ann was sitting in a chair in the centre of the room, a heap of tattered, soggy paper handkerchiefs at her feet. She wasn't actively crying at the moment, just snuffling occasionally, her hands shredding a Kleenex restlessly. Crystal perched on the arm of her chair, an expression of concern on her face, and a full box of Kleenex on her lap. As Lou-Ann let the shredded one fall to the floor, she pulled out a fresh one and handed it to her automatically. It should have been a funny routine but, looking at Lou-Ann's red blotchy face, it wasn't.

Uncle No'ccount leaned against the farther wall, watching them unhappily. His fingers caressed the harmonica, probably he itched to play it. Equally probably, he felt it wouldn't show proper respect for Lou-Ann's anxiety. He nodded to me and sketched a brief salute with the harmonica.

Bart stood by the window, looking intently down into the street. He seemed to have dissociated himself from everyone present, although it was his suite. He didn't even turn round when I spoke.

'Is there anything I can do?'

Lou-Ann raised her head and looked at me pleadingly. 'Find her, Douglas. She's lost—she's lost and gone—' She broke off, her head cocked, as though to catch an echo of something she could not quite place. (*'You are lost and gone for ever, Oh, my darling, Clementine'.*) Fortunately for her peace of mind, the fragment of lyric drifted away.

'You know your way around this city, Douglas,' she continued, after the brief pause. 'Where could she be?'

'Has anyone called the police?' I asked.

'No—and nobody's going to.' Bart turned away from the window, his shoulders hunched menacingly. 'We don't want no police nosing around here, boy.' He glanced sideways at Lou-Ann. 'It wouldn't be good publicity for the Act. You know how Maw would hate that.'

'That's right,' Lou-Ann agreed reluctantly. 'Maw wouldn't want bad publicity. But—'

'You jes' leave things be for a little while longer,' Bart said. 'She'll maybe turn up by herself when she feels like it. You never know—she might just be out on a tear.'

'Maw don't drink!' Crystal sounded genuinely shocked. 'Leastwise, not that much.'

'How do *you* know what she mighta decided to do last night? Was you with her?'

'No—no, Bart.' Crystal lost colour.

'She was with me, Bart,' Lou-Ann said mechanically. 'She was playing gin rummy.'

'Yeah?' Bart glanced at her suspiciously. 'Going in quite a lot for card games these nights, ain't you? Maybe I should look in for a hand or two sometimes.'

'Why don't you, Bart?' Lou-Ann turned to him eagerly. For the moment, her mother was forgotten in the place of her bigger, more enduring problem. 'You ain't been by in quite a long spell. Maybe we could sit by ourselves and talk awhile.'

Bart ignored her, returning to his vigil at the window, staring intently down into the street. Was he more worried than he seemed? Lou-Ann sniffed unappealingly, and Crystal, still wary of Bart, passed her another Kleenex.

'Where's Sam?' I spoke over their heads to Uncle No'ccount who, at least, seemed to be keeping calm, if not neutral, in the face of this situation.

'Checking the hospitals,' Uncle No'ccount said.

'Been gone a coupla hours now. Seems like there's an awful lot of hospitals in London.'

There were quite a few morgues, too, but it wasn't a thought to voice aloud. Uncle No'ccount nodded at me glumly, as though he had caught the vibrations of that thought. 'Don't seem like good sense to go rushing around like a hen with its head cut off. We can't tell which ones he's been to until he gets back to tell us. Then maybe you can think of some others we might try. Not the police, though.' His voice was firm. 'Not yet.'

It was the other half of Public Relations. There are things to be seized upon and publicized for more than they're worth. And there are things to be hushed up— usually the things that would get you the most publicity, but the wrong kind. A few police inquiries here and there, and the story of the Client's private predilections might be discovered. So, the police were out.

And if some frightened, bewildered lady were roaming around an unknown city with a case of amnesia, well, that was just too bad—for her. She'd just have to continue roaming around, until she either remembered at last or until one of us caught up with her and told her. The Client must be protected.

Meanwhile, the Client was glaring down into the street with a burning intensity. Willing Maw Cooney to come back to the bosom of her loving Troupe? Somehow, I doubted it. I moved up behind him and followed the direction of his eyes.

The attraction was instantly obvious. They stood waiting at the bus stop, twittering together, in the shortest mini-skirts I'd seen in months. Not birds, fledgelings definitely. Out of school uniform for the afternoon, probably. Not much older than thirteen.

The Client exhaled a deep breath. 'Man,' he said softly, 'ain't they something?'

That was when the policeman knocked on the door.

He was a very young constable. He moved into the room, looking very unhappy. Perhaps the Police School had warned him there'd be days like this. Someone ought to ask him for directions to put him at his ease, but I wasn't up to it. He saw Lou-Ann's red-rimmed eyes and the pile of soiled Kleenex at her feet, and retreated half a pace. He seemed to be wishing they'd handed him a simple assignment, like straightening out a three-mile traffic snarl-up at Hyde Park Corner.

Lou-Ann rose to her feet and advanced upon him. 'Maw?' she said, her voice breaking. 'You've come about Maw?' Crystal moved with her, and Uncle No'ccount came forward swiftly.

The constable winced, but stood firm as they approached. He'd be worth his weight in riot duty some day. Trying to by-pass the women, he spoke across them to Uncle No'ccount.

'I'm terribly sorry. Perhaps I could speak to you in private, sir.'

'She's *my* mother,' Lou-Ann challenged him. 'Tell *me*. Where is she? Is she all right? Does she have amnesia—?'

It was obviously worse than the constable had thought it was going to be. Too much showed in his face. Lou-Ann didn't miss any of it.

'She's hurt!' she shrieked. 'What happened? Where is she? Let me go to her!'

'Take it easy, honey.' Crystal put an arm around her. Uncle No'ccount glanced, with some pity, at the young constable. Bart still looked out of the window, indifferent to the scene in the room. Yet he was listening.

'She's in Charing Cross Hospital.' Perhaps they have a formula for these things. If so, the young constable had forgotten it. He blurted out the information. 'It was a traffic accident. On the Embankment. Yesterday afternoon.'

'Yesterday afternoon! But—'

'There was no identification,' he defended. 'We weren't able to trace her immediately. We just knew, from her clothes, that she was an American.'

'No identification!' Unable to bear anything else, Lou-Ann pounced on a detail. 'But she had her passport, and her wallet with lots of membership cards, and there must have been plenty of letters in her purse, too.'

'There was no purse—no handbag,' he said. 'Nothing at the scene. We think it possible that someone picked it up and took it away. People do that sometimes,' he said sadly. 'You may get it back later—with the money missing.'

'Anyhow, you've found us,' Uncle No'ccount said. 'That must mean she's been able to talk and tell you.'

Bart swung away from the window and faced into the room. His eyes were narrowed against the change of light. He waited for the answer.

'Er, yes,' the constable said unconvincingly. 'That is,' he qualified, 'she hadn't regained consciousness fully. But she said a few things—wandering a bit—and we were able to interpret them. Actually, we took rather a chance. I came to see if you knew anything about her, and then, of course, from your reactions—'

'Then she ain't "actually"—' Bart mimicked the accent—'awake and in her right mind. Maybe you better tell us just how bad she is.'

'I couldn't say.' The constable had had enough. He wasn't a diagnostician, and he didn't intend to be. His own duties were bad enough. 'Perhaps you might come along to the hospital and identify her,' he suggested. 'We presume the lady is one of your party, but we'd like to be sure. Although she must be, there *can't* be two middle-aged American ladies missing on the same day.'

But there could, and a sudden loss of colour in his face showed that he had just realized this. The young constable was having a rough initiation into the seamier side of his job. It was all very well to join the Force with happy visions of disarming bank robbers in unarmed combat and rescuing children from burning buildings, but he was beginning to realize that a large part of his time might be spent in trying to cope with intractable people who got themselves into unhealthy predicaments—and their relatives, who would somehow assume that it was all his fault because he hadn't had the foresight to prevent it. He looked as though he were having second thoughts about remaining one of our Brave Boys in Blue. But he pulled himself together.

'I think we should go to the hospital,' he said firmly. 'After you've made the formal identification, it will be a lot simpler. Perhaps,' he added craftily, 'you might like to have her moved to a private room, or engage special nurses.'

'You mean she isn't being taken care of?' All the American bugaboos about the National Health Service, fostered by years of propaganda from the American Medical Association, rose to terrify Lou-Ann. And, more practically, to give her a jolt of adrenalin to get her moving. She bolted for the door. The rest of us followed.

The constable was right. It could only have been Maw Cooney, and it was. But he'd glossed over how badly she'd been hurt. Screens were around the bed when we approached and, meeting Uncle No'ccount's eyes, I could see that I wasn't the only one who knew there wasn't going to be time to carry out all the orders Lou-Ann was shouting. There would be no private room, no specialist from Harley Street, no round-the-clock nurses.

We stood around the bed, more for Lou-Ann's sake than for Maw's. The pale face on the pillow grew paler, the breathing more stertorous. After about half an hour, she opened her eyes, but she didn't see any of us.

'That bastard pushed me!' she said loudly, and died.

CHAPTER IX

IT WASN'T EVIDENCE. Perhaps it wasn't anything stronger than the antipathy I felt for this whole assignment. I looked round at the others.

Uncle No'ccount's eyes were downcast. Whatever he thought, he was going to keep it to himself. Crystal's attention was centred on Lou-Ann—probably she had paid no attention to Maw Cooney's last words, only to the fact that they were the last, and the effect this would have on Lou-Ann.

Lou-Ann was sobbing loudly. The constable was frowning with impersonal, rueful concern—it meant nothing to him. Obviously, he assumed that any lady who had been pushed under a moving vehicle was entitled to a little leeway in referring to her pusher. He didn't realize she travelled around with a home-grown matched set of bastards. He thought it was just any old bastard she was referring to.

Then Sam found us. Approaching hesitantly, he took in the situation at a glance, and wasted no time. 'Baby! Sweetheart!' He swept Lou-Ann into his arms. 'Baby!'

And that was something else I should have known. Or noticed. His wild enthusiasm for her abilities, his unconcern for the problems of Perkins & Tate, his cold loathing for the Client. Yes, there's nothing like a little hindsight after the penny has dropped.

'There, there, baby,' he crooned, his arms around her, his cheeks against hers, rocking her gently.

It stirred the Client to action. He grabbed for Lou-Ann's wrist and tugged her away from Sam. She came unresisting, not even noticing what was happening. Her gawkiness, the awkward impression she gave of being all knees and elbows, was gone now, dissolved in grief.

The Client lifted her, and she lay back, fluid, in his arms, like some Art Nouveau poster updated in modern dress. He looked down at her, his eyes cold behind the mask of concern on his face.

'Ain't nothing more we can do here,' he said. 'We're going back to the hotel.'

'Maw—' she struggled feebly.

'Nothing to do with us, now,' he said. 'We'll leave Sam and Doug to take care of things here—that's what we pay them for.'

He had to get that in. Sam's face tightened. It didn't matter to me. I felt strongly that I'd much rather be the Client's employee than his friend—or his wife. It was the nastiest afterthought I'd had in a long time, and it didn't bear close examination.

The Client swung towards the exit, carrying Lou-Ann. 'Come on,' he snapped over his shoulder. Crystal hesitated a moment, then followed them out.

Uncle No'ccount looked after them thoughtfully, then closed ranks with Sam and me. 'This is a terrible thing,' he said. 'What do we do now?'

It was a very good question. Too bad I didn't have a very good answer—or any answer at all. Fortunately, the ball wasn't in my court this time.

'There'll be an inquest,' the young constable said. 'We'll let you know. Just routine in a traffic accident. The chap stopped, after all. Not as though it were really his fault. He had the green light. There was a crowd of people waiting at the kerb. She just shot out in front of him before he could brake. People pushing, jostling, impatient—' He shrugged.

That summed it up nicely. Crowds at the kerb—probably most of them foreigners—an American woman who wasn't used to the traffic being on the left, a moment's carelessness, uncertain footing, perhaps jostling from behind—and another tourist bit the dust. The police were used to it.

Especially in the West End. In the height of the tourist season. Tourists were increasingly essential to the economy. They were also, as reflected in the young constable's face, a bloody nuisance. They trailed around asking stupid questions, they complained about perfectly good service, they fell over their own feet and broke vital bones, they stepped in front of buses, they turned on gas fires and forgot to light them, they had heart attacks, they had premature babies. And, sometimes, they murdered each other.

But there was no evidence.

I looked at Sam, at Uncle No'ccount, at the constable. Their faces were grave and shuttered, each preoccupied with what this death would involve for him personally. For the constable, the police routine which would end in a verdict of misadventure. For Sam, the red tape, the temperament, the transatlantic telephone calls, the explanations—perhaps, even, some of the heartbreak—standing by, watching Lou-Ann suffer, without the right to comfort her.

For Uncle No'ccount—I glanced at him again, realizing how very little I knew about him. Not even whether my earlier suspicions, born of the Cousins' sly remarks, about his feelings for Maw Cooney were true. His hair was disturbed, as though at some moment he had swept his hand through it to remove a hat he hadn't been wearing. Slowly, in his own world, he brought the harmonica to his lips and began to play. It was a dirge, a soft mourning wail for everything that had been and that could never be. As a tribute, it was as good as sending a bouquet—and a lot more personal.

'Please! I can't have you disturbing the other patients!' A nurse came whirling around the edge of the screens, facing us fiercely, prepared to do battle for the living—as she must. Maw Cooney was beyond her help.

'I'm sorry, ma'am.' Uncle No'ccount lowered the harmonica, seemingly still in the daze of his own private world. 'I didn't mean to disturb nobody. I just didn't rightly think.'

'Come on,' Sam said abruptly. 'Let's get out of here.'

Back at the hotel, Sam led us directly to Lou-Ann's room. The door was ajar and I would have hesitated about entering, largely because I hate to face a woman in tears, but Sam barged ahead. More slowly, Uncle No'ccount and I followed.

Sam had halted, just inside the door. An open suitcase was on one of the twin beds, partly packed. The room already had a bare and impersonal feeling. I noticed a vaguely familiar look to some of the clothing spread on the bed beside the suitcase—the garments had belonged to Maw Cooney. There was nothing in the room to mark Lou-Ann's passage.

The bathroom door opened, and Crystal came out, carrying a toothbrush, sponge bag, and oddments of cosmetics. She halted upon seeing us, curiously defensive. 'Well, it's got to be done,' she said. 'Better sooner than later—and there's nobody else to do it. I mean, you can't expect poor Lou-Ann to.'

Sam seemed ready to argue the point. 'Where *is* Lou-Ann?' he demanded.

'She's gone.' More defensive than ever, Crystal refused to meet his eyes. 'Bart's moved her in with him. They're up in his suite now.'

Sam turned white. Over his head, Crystal and Uncle No'ccount exchanged glances. So, Sam's feelings were common knowledge to the Troupe. I was the only mug who hadn't known—but then, I had walked in in the middle of the film.

'I reckon you can go up, if'n you want,' Crystal said. 'I don't expect they'll mind.'

Sam turned on his heel and raced out. Crystal and Uncle No'ccount communed silently for another moment. Uncertain of where my post ought to be, I lingered.

'Is there anything I can do?' I asked. Why do you always feel like the third head on a two-headed calf at moments like these?

'I reckon not.' Crystal smiled faintly. 'Thank you, though. I take your offer mighty kindly. I know Lou-Ann will, too.'

That seemed to be my dismissal. As well as my marching orders. If I read it correctly, I was expected to go upstairs and make the same useless offer of assistance to Lou-Ann. There never was anything one could do—unless, perhaps, just *being* there was doing enough.

I was aware, as I went out, that Uncle No'ccount had moved forward to start folding some of the garments on the bed and lay them gently in the suitcase . . .

Sam opened the door. He hadn't regained any colour, and he didn't seem very pleased to see me. 'I thought you were the doctor,' he said, stepping back to let me in.

The Client was lounging against the window, looking down, but his heart wasn't in it. Lou-Ann was nowhere in sight.

'Where is she?' I asked.

'I put her to bed.' The Client moved away from his vantage point. 'She was pretty cut-up—and she's got a show to do tonight. Sam, here, phoned down for a doctor for her. I suppose it can't do her any harm. You want to see her? Reckon *that* can't do no harm, neither.'

'No, I won't disturb her,' I said. 'I just came along to see if there was anything I could do.'

'Not much nobody can do—time like this.' The Client moved restlessly towards the window again, but abandoned the idea after a brief glance out.

'You'll be able to help *me*,' Sam said. 'There'll be all kinds of red tape over this. You'll know what to do.'

I refrained from pointing out that Perkins & Tate clients weren't in the habit of dying on them. 'You'll probably have to do something about the American Embassy, for a start,' I suggested helpfully. 'I think they're supposed to be notified in cases like this.'

'Cases like *what*?' The Client whirled on me, looking ready to fight.

'Sudden death,' I said. 'One of their Nationals dying in a foreign country. I think it comes under their jurisdiction. They might be able to help with the red tape, too.'

'Oh, yuh.' Losing interest, he turned away. His restless pacing carried him past the window again and again, the view failed to hold him.

There was a knock at the door. Casually, while Sam was leading the doctor through to see Lou-Ann, I strolled over to the window myself and checked. It was a lot more interesting for me than it was for Bart. So far as he was concerned, there were just a couple of middle-aged ladies waiting at the bus stop—they must have been getting on for twenty-two.

'She hasn't been able to sleep, she can't even stop crying.' Sam came back into the room with the bulletin, as though it might be of interest to someone. It left Bart even more indifferent than the scene beneath the window. Then he seemed to notice that Sam was expecting some reaction.

'That's sure too bad.' Almost visibly, he pulled himself together. 'Poor kid.'

'I can see it's just breaking your heart.' Sam eyed him with distaste.

A nasty light flared in Bart's eyes, then dimmed as the doctor came out of Lou-Ann's room. The doctor was heading towards Sam, but Bart intercepted him.

'How is she, Doc?' He did it well. He was humble, anxious, unmistakably the worried husband.

I wondered if the act would have impressed me if I hadn't disliked him so thoroughly. His shoulders were slumped forward, his mouth drooped, pulling his face into the proper lines of unhappiness, but his eyes were watchful and calculating. Even so, it would have registered with the right impact in a photo.

The doctor responded to it immediately. Bart took his arm and drew him over to a corner as he started to answer. We were left outside the consultation. But we weren't going to let him get away with that. Sam and I exchanged glances, then bore down on them. Sam wanted to hear about Lou-Ann—and I had my own reasons for wanting to know what was being said in that corner.

'. . . great shock, naturally,' the doctor was saying.

Bart nodded, the impatience only visible to those who knew him. 'But you've given her something?' he insisted.

'Yes, you needn't worry. She'll sleep—'

'Sleep!' Bart interrupted. 'She can't go to sleep now! Didn't nobody tell you who we are? We've got a show to give tonight. If'n you want her to sleep, then you give her some pills to take later on. But she's got to be awake for the performance. We got a Public to think of. Don't you know "The Show Must Go On"?'

The doctor backed away from the vehemence of Bart's protest. A certain reserve shuttered his face as he began to get the picture. 'I think—'

'It's all right, Bart,' Lou-Ann stood in the doorway. 'I remembered about the show. I didn't take the pills he gave me. I can go on tonight.'

'Good girl!' Bart crossed to put his arms around her, a split second before Sam could reach her. She clung to him shakily. 'I knowed you was a Trouper. But—' he glared at Sam—'that doc shoulda been briefed not to give you nothing that might slow you down.'

'She shouldn't go on,' Sam said stubbornly. 'She should take those pills and go to bed. The show can go on without her for a couple of nights.'

'Is that so?' Bart grinned wolfishly. 'I thought you was the one who figured she was so good the show could go on without anybody *but* her. You're sure changing your tune fast.'

'These are special circumstances, and she shouldn't—'

'I'll go on, Bart.' Lou-Ann seemed in a daze, but she was still fighting. 'I'll make them laugh tonight, Bart. Honest, I will.'

'Sure, you will, kid.' He hugged her, enjoying Sam's face as he did so. 'You'll be great.'

She was terrible, of course. She flung herself around like a demented rag doll—except that she was flesh-and-blood, and her timing was off. She seemed likely to do herself a permanent injury, rather than make the audience laugh.

The audience felt it, too. They heard the heavy thud as she hit the floor without breaking her fall properly. It upset them, without their knowing why, and they resented it. There had been no publicity yet—so they didn't know they were seeing a Gallant Little Trouper. They just thought it was a bad performance. And the feeling was getting through to Lou-Ann onstage, driving her to more drastic mugging, more frantic gymnastics.

Sam was suffering with—and for—her. 'She ought to take it easier.' He clutched my arm during a particularly dicey pratfall. 'She'll never make it through the week, if she goes on at this rate. I don't give a damn what Bart says—after tonight, she's out of the show until she pulls herself together.'

'Okay, but who'll bell the cat?' I murmured. Bart had come onstage now, standing in the background like a great black panther, brooding on the scene. As the amplifiers throbbed out the familiar beat, he stepped into the spotlight.

'*Homesteader, Homesteader,*
   '*Ridin' alone . . .*'

The audience went wild. Wilder than usual. After the embarrassment of the always corny, but now inept, comedy routine, the dark magnetic figure singing the hit song of the moment provided release and exhilaration. I doubted that he would allow Lou-Ann to take any time off, now that she was so bad. The worse the others were, the better he looked by comparison—and he knew it. You could call the Client a lot of things—but not one of them was 'fool'.

'She's got to knock off and go home *now.*' Sam leaned forward in his seat, straining to look into the wings, where Lou-Ann's small slight figure slumped against the wall in dejection. 'Come on, I'm going to take her home.'

We were in aisle seats, but we had to fight our way through a crowd of standees to get to the door leading backstage. I was aware of the Client's cold eyes following our progress from the stage. People didn't walk out when he was singing—especially not his Road Manager and his PRO. We'd pay for this defection later.

We hadn't quite reached Lou-Ann when the Client ended his number and held up his hand to quell the audience. 'Now, folks,' he said, 'I'd like a big hand for a real little Trouper. Y'all don't know what it cost her to come out here tonight and give you a show.' He gestured to Lou-Ann and she moved forward on to the stage.

Sam tried to stop her, but she brushed past him. Any

time, anywhere, any actress will climb over a mountain of corpses to take an extra bow—and Lou-Ann wasn't going to be done out of this one.

'Yessir.' Bart put his arm around her, displaying her to the audience like a prize specimen. 'This brave little lady came here tonight, even though her heart was sure-enough breaking, just so as not to disappoint all you lovely people. You see, her poor darling mother—beloved of us all, I might add—died today. In a traffic accident.'

There it was again—one of the things I had learned to dread in the States. The appalling American habit—elevated into a virtue by the jest plain folks, hell, jest plain *honest* folks' type—of hauling out their bleeding guts and holding them aloft for attention and admiration.

By rights, the audience should have shrunk from it. But your reticent Englishman feels that reticence should apply only to himself—he doesn't worry overmuch about what *you* want to give away. And it was certainly adding something to the show tonight. Just ask any typical member of an audience about the most memorable performance he ever saw. Some of them will choose Olivier or Gielgud, but nine out of ten—being jest plain honest folks—will plump for the night the juvenile lead fell into the orchestra pit, fracturing his femur, dislocating three vertebrae, lacerating his skull, and had to be carried off, streaming with blood.

They applauded with wild enthusiasm, and Lou-Ann took her bows proudly. Bart still had his arm around her, as though he were never going to let her go again. Certainly he wasn't going to let her back out of any performance while he could get this reaction from an audience. They milked the applause for all it was worth, then Bart held up his hand again.

'I'd like all of you to know that I'm working on a new song now that's going to be a tribute to Maw, and tell all about how she cheered us on through the dark days we've had, and how much she meant to us all. But until I get that finished, I'd like to sort of "make do" with somebody else's song, which kinda fits the occasion.'

The Cousins had evidently been briefed ahead. They picked up the downbeat and gave him an intro. Perhaps I was the only one offstage who noticed that Uncle No'ccount had lowered his harmonica, bowed his head, and dissociated himself from the proceedings. For a moment, I wondered whether he might not know the tune, then I realized that even I knew the tune. In that case, Uncle No'cccount had more taste than I had ever given him credit for.

The song was that great old tearjerker, 'In The Baggage Car Ahead'. All about the grave little girl who is sitting all alone in the train steaming southwards towards her home and, when a kindly stranger asks her where her mother is, the child replies, 'In The Baggage Car Ahead'.

I had never seen anyone do it before, but Sam was actually gnashing his teeth. He snarled out several words, any one of which his own dear mother would have flattened him with the back of her hand for. 'I'll kill that bastard,' he grated. 'I'll kill him.'

But the Client wasn't the type to be killed. He was a predator, not a victim. Sam must know that. Just as he must know that, with a solid English success under Bart's belt, he must go on building Bart for the Agency. His personal feelings didn't come under any heading on the Agency's Balance Sheet, so they weren't worth considering. Not even by Sam. That was the worst of it—the bright New American Dream held no place for emotions. It measured success by the bankroll, the ratings, the wall-to-wall broads and broadloom. The golden eggs were beginning to roll now, so the Goose was sacrosanct. Nobody would kill him—they'd kill themselves first, trying to quash indictments, wallpapering over murky stains from the past, and turning a blind eye to the future. Our Boy Bart had it made now.

The song ended, and Bart took his bow. Lou-Ann, tears streaming down her face, took a bow, too. I felt sick. But what else could you expect? Maw Cooney had brought her up to curry favour with an audience at any price. All Lou-Ann knew was that applause said that they were loving her. For the wrong reasons—but they were loving her. She bowed again.

'Come on,' I said to Sam. 'I'll buy you a drink.'

CHAPTER X

GERRY HAD been there when I got back to the flat, and I had filled him in on everything except my private suspicions. He had promised to turn his hand to the wheel, and take the early morning tour of duty at the hotel, leaving me to cope with some of the office routine for a change of pace—and peace and quiet.

When I woke, he had already left. By the time I'd dressed, eaten and shaved, Penny had arrived for work. 'Feeling better?' she asked.

'Yes, thank you.' She didn't look at me. At least she had come back. I was grateful for that.

She settled down with a pair of scissors and began going through the pile of morning papers. Her composure slipped away. 'How awful,' she said. 'Oh, that poor girl.'

I nodded, without telling her that she didn't know the half of it. When the Client had chosen to make his announcement to a crowded house from the stage, the resultant coverage wasn't too surprising.

The earliest editions just had it as a Stop Press item. Some of the later editions had pulled out the first publicity shots we had sent them, and were running totally unsuitable pictures of Lou-Ann in 'comedy costume' along with the bare outlines of the story. All of them were obviously set to give the story the fullest coverage in later editions. Unless we were exceptionally lucky and some political figure got assassinated, or war broke out, we were doomed to have the full glare of a publicity spotlight on the Troupe—with all the nasty ramifications that that might entail.

In a way, it was almost poetic justice. After all, The Client had brought it on himself.

Unfortunately, it was Perkins & Tate's job to stop it. And we couldn't rely on luck. I cursed Gerry for not ringing me immediately to liaise and plan action, then wondered just what he *was* doing. Perhaps he was already in The Street, trying to pick up the pieces.

'Run down and get the very latest editions,' I ordered Penny. 'All you can find. Try Charing Cross Station.'

I tossed her a pound note and she turned and ran. She was a nice kid, if a little literal-minded. Then I sat back and destroyed a couple of fingernails with a thoroughness that would have done credit to Sam, while I waited for her to return with the papers.

When she did, Bart was with her. He carried the pile of newspapers, crowding on her heels, leering down at her. She looked pale and frightened. I felt a bit pale myself.

'Y'oughta take better care of this little gal than sending her out alone.' He tossed the papers down on the desk in front of me. 'I don't like the way some of them characters around the station was staring at her.'

'I don't like it myself,' I said pointedly.

'Then you shouldn't send her over there. It was just a good thing I happened to come along and find her.' He tried to toss an arm around her shoulders, but she eluded him, moving to the file and taking out a folder we hadn't used in months, busying herself with it.

'Ain't she cute?' Bart chuckled at me. 'Honey,' he leaned over her, as though to study the file, 'you jest pay attention to your Uncle Bart, now, when he tells you—'

'How's your wife?' I interrupted.

He straightened up. 'Huh?' he said blankly.

'Your wife,' I said. 'You remember—Lou-Ann?'

'Oh, yuh,' his face fell into the smooth unctuous lines of concern. 'Poor kid, poor kid. I'm really worried about her, you know. She ain't taking this at all well—'

'How well should you take it when your mother dies?'

'Well, sure, I understand that. Why, Maw—' he reached up and swept off his sombrero, holding it over his heart and bowing his head—'Maw, she was like a mother to us all. It's plumb broke me up, too. You jest don't know how much Maw meant to me.'

About a fifteen-year stretch in the Federal Penitentiary, I'd have said. But he didn't know I knew that. It seemed to me that there was something else I knew, but it was lost among the other niggling worries at the back of my mind.

'Of course, she meant even more to Lou-Ann,' he went on. 'They was as close as could be. That's why I'm so worried about Lou-Ann now—'

A paper fluttered from the file to the floor, and Penny bent to pick it up. Bart watched her, losing his train of thought for a moment, then recovered.

'Lou-Ann, she really depended on her Maw for everything. And it don't seem like she's never going to stop crying no more. I sure wish there was something I could do to help her.'

'Why don't you try cutting the sob stuff out of the show,' I suggested. 'Drop "In The Baggage Car Ahead", and forget about putting in any tribute stuff. Just carry on with the show as you've been doing it.'

'No tribute to Maw?' He looked genuinely shocked. 'Why, that wouldn't hardly be seemly. What do you think we are?'

I could have told him, but it would only have led to bloodshed. 'It wouldn't do any harm to forget it.'

'Why don't we go out to lunch and talk it over, like?' He was staring at Penny hungrily. '*All* of us. I'd sure be interested to know the opinions of the President of the Black Bart Fan Club on this subject.'

Penny's mouth tightened grimly and I suspected that, like mine, her opinions could lead to bloodshed, too.

'I'm afraid we're going to be busy for lunch,' I said hastily. 'All this publicity you got with your announcement last night.' Penny shot me a grateful glance. 'We've got to get busy on the follow-ups for it.'

It was the one subject which could have diverted him. He looked at the pile of newspapers complacently. 'Sure did set the cat among the pigeons, didn't I? You reckon I oughta follow it up with something dramatic—like a reward offered for catching the reckless driver?'

'It wasn't exactly hit-and-run,' I reminded him coldly. 'The driver stopped. The police have all his particulars. If you try a stunt like that, you could find yourself in the middle of the biggest libel suit of the century.'

'Oh.' He deflated slowly. 'Hell, it was jest a thought.'

'Think again,' I said. There was no one I'd rather see up to his neck in hot water but, unfortunately, he was still the Client. And it would reflect back on Perkins &

Tate. For that reason only, he had to be protected from himself.

'Then how about—?'

'How about going back to the hotel?' I said. 'Get everyone together, and I'll come along for a council of war in a couple of hours—after I get everything sorted out here.'

'I don't know. I think—' He was prepared to be obstinate, and I was afraid I knew the reason why.

'You go ahead.' With a silent shrug of apology at Penny, I sold her down the river. '*We'll* be along shortly.'

Black Bart might not have been the greatest star since the Roaring Twenties, but he certainly had the entourage mentality. 'Where *is* everybody?' he demanded.

I looked around, observing them carefully—still not quite willing to admit, even to myself, what I was looking for. (Bastard, bastard, which one was the biggest bastard of all?)

Lou-Ann perched wanly on the edge of the big chair. The Cousins sprawled by the fireplace, engaged in a desultory game of craps. Sam and Gerry were worrying over a Press Release in the corner. I had promised Penny an extra three pounds a week 'danger money' and sworn that either Gerry or I would always be along whenever she had to see the Client, so she was here with me now.

Bart hovered near the window, occasionally moving forward to pat Lou-Ann's shoulder—when he remembered that he was supposed to be a comfort to his grieving wife. But he always returned to the window, although he never seemed to see what he was hoping for. And his eyes kept sliding to Penny in a way that made me feel like a pimp for having brought her along.

'Where *is* everybody?' Bart repeated. There were only two people missing.

'I think Crystal's gone shopping, Bart,' Lou-Ann said softly. 'I asked her to get some things for me. She oughta be back soon.'

'Yeah?' Bart said. 'And where's that lazy, no'ccount old fool with the harmonica? Why ain't he around?'

'Maybe he's gone to church,' I said. 'After a death—*some* people pray.'

'Pray!' Black Bart exploded into laughter. 'Hell, boy, there ain't been no Revival Meeting lately!' He staggered with laughter to the fireplace, and swayed over the Cousins, pointing down at them. 'That's the only time *my* kinda people get down on their knees.' He scooped up the dice, leaving the Cousins hovering there, uncertainly.

He shook the dice and flung them from him. They swirled across the carpet and hit the leg of Lou-Ann's chair. A single dot stared upwards from each one.

'You see that?' Bart crowed. 'Snake eyes! That's the only eyes you got looking at you. What you talking like that for, then—you understudying Billy Graham? Nobody's watching—only old Snake Eyes. So you jest grab what you want afore you're too old and dead to enjoy it.'

Silence hung in the room a minute. Lou-Ann seemed to shrink. Sam moved as though to go to her, but hesitated. Losing interest, Bart whirled and went back to the window. After another silent moment, Cousin Homer slithered across the carpet and retrieved the dice.

The crap game continued, but some of its zest was missing.

'Please,' Penny whispered to me, 'I'd like to go home.'

'In a minute,' I whispered back. It was still ominously quiet. The first person to draw attention by a decisive word or movement might yet unleash another storm.

When the door of the suite opened, it seemed that it was to be Uncle No'ccount who was to receive the brunt of Bart's still unspent mood. As though he sensed this, he advanced into the room diffidently.

Bart moved to meet him. 'Where the hell have you been?' he snarled.

'Workin,' Bart.' Placatingly, he held out a worn loose-leaf binder to Bart, like an offering. 'Working hard. All day.'

'You jest *better* have been!' Bart snatched the binder and disappeared into his bedroom, slamming the door behind him.

The atmosphere lightened immediately. The crap game grew noisier, and Uncle No'ccount wandered over to join the Cousins. I nodded to Penny and she folded up her shorthand notebook, to slip away while the going was good.

She nearly collided with Crystal, who was entering as she exited. They did a little side-stepping waltz in the doorway, then Crystal smiled faintly and stood aside. Penny rushed past as though all the hounds of hell were behind her. Crystal's smile faded, replaced by a faint frown as she looked after Penny. She came into the room, and was visibly relieved to see it full of people.

It occurred to me that Crystal could not have entirely escaped a certain amount of backlash from Bart's various episodes.

Lou-Ann looked up then and saw Crystal. She beckoned and Crystal crossed to her—I noticed that she was carrying no parcels. She crouched beside Lou-Ann's chair and the two of them whispered together urgently.

I stood up, deciding to join Sam and Gerry. But, as I turned, I found Cousin Zeke had detached himself from the crap game and was at my elbow, staring at me plaintively.

'I hear tell they're gonna get Maw cremated,' he said.

I hadn't heard, but it seemed like a sensible thing to do. 'Not until after the inquest, I imagine,' I said.

'That means we ain't gonna go home, then? Means we jest gonna stay here jest the same? Take the ashes with us when we go back?' His voice rose on a progressively querulous note. 'It don't seem right.'

'After all, you have contracts to fulfil,' I reminded him. 'And it couldn't make any difference to Mrs Cooney now, could it?' Belatedly, I remembered that it might make a lot of difference to him. 'How are you feeling?'

'Not too good.' He glanced at me warily. 'Not as bad as I *might*, but not too good.'

'The new pills the doctor gave you are working all right, are they?'

'Yeah,' he admitted cautiously. 'I guess maybe it's partly that. And partly, I was wondering—' He looked towards Lou-Ann and lowered his voice. 'Do you think it mighta been maybe the Conjure Woman got things a little bit mixed up?'

'Mixed up?' For a moment, I didn't follow him.

'Yeah. You think maybe that old Conjure Woman jest seen that *somebody* died when we was away from home? Maybe she couldn't rightly make out *who*. An', since my ma was asking her about me, maybe she jest reckoned it musta been *me* as was gonna die. But maybe she made a mistake, and it was really Maw Cooney all the time.'

'That's a very good theory. You hold on to it.' It wasn't much of a brand to snatch from the burning mess but, if Cousin Zeke could get over his neurosis, it might ease the situation a bit.

Or was that the whole idea? An insane thought flooded into my brain. Had Cousin Zeke painstakingly worked this out beforehand—and had *he* pushed Maw into the path of that speeding car so that a death *would* occur away from home? A sacrifice to his Conjure Gods in place of himself? It was a crazy notion—but no crazier than some of the notions I'd heard from these characters.

'I really think you have the solution there,' I said weakly. I only hoped I hadn't.

'On the other hand—' he wasn't to be comforted for long—'maybe Maw's dying was jest extra-like. Maybe it was something that old Conjure Woman didn't never see at all. So maybe I'm still a-gonna die while we're all away from home. 'Course, if that happens, that means there'll have to be another one die, too. Kinda thing always comes in threes.' He looked around the room with gloomy relish, obviously speculating on the identity of the third victim.

'I'm sure you were right the first time,' I said hastily. 'The Conjure Woman misinterpreted her . . . um, facts.

There was only one death—and it was Maw Cooney's. You're going to be all right.'

He nodded dubiously and shuffled back to the crap game, having shot his bolt and left me transfixed by it. The idea of a series of three deaths had unnerved me completely.

After a moment, I pulled myself together, mentally cursing Cousin Zeke, the Conjure Woman, Maw Cooney and the day I ever got mixed up with this entire bunch of lunatics. I had never thought I'd feel nostalgic about dear old Cinecittà, but I was beginning to remember it as a golden period in my life. Ah, for those happy, carefree days of shrieking tantrums over billing, and those merry evenings spent trailing starlets along the path of *la dolce vita*, trying to drag them back to their hotels so that they wouldn't photograph with bags under their eyes in the morning. I didn't appreciate a soft job when I had it.

I wondered if Gerry felt that way, too. Certainly, from the expression on his face, he had taken just about enough of whatever Sam was handing him. I went over to them, ready to act as peacemaker, if necessary.

As I reached them, the bedroom door opened. Black Bart stood in the doorway, surveying the room. He glowered sombrely at everyone, not missing the fact that Crystal had returned, then looked round again restlessly.

'Where *is* everybody?' he demanded.

'We're all here, Bart,' Lou-Ann said.

'No, you ain't,' Bart said. His eye fell on me. 'You, boy,' he said. 'Where's your secretary-kid? I'm outa cigarettes. I want her to go fetch me some.'

'She's gone for the day,' I said. 'She only works part-time.'

'What'd you let her go for? You mighta knowed we'd want something.'

'I'll get your cigarettes,' I said coldly. 'What brand do you smoke?'

'How do I know? All your junk tastes alike to me. Jest get me half a dozen packs. We got a rehearsing session comin' up now.'

As I left the suite, I heard him expending more wrath on the Cousins.

'You bastards think I brought you over here to enjoy yourselves? Git your guitars and let's make like you're gonna do something to earn your keep. We wanta rehearse my new number for the show tonight.'

BACKSTAGE at the theatre, I took the first chance I had had to sit down in hours. Bart had deliberately kept me on the hop all afternoon. Pointedly, on errands one would normally expect an office junior to do: post a letter, bring in coffee, get more cigarettes, go for the evening papers. It was deliberate punishment for having let Penny go home. I knew it—and he had intended that I know it. I had held my temper, ignored the snickers of the Cousins, and the sympathy of Uncle No'ccount and the girls. I didn't need the anxious pleading in Sam's face to keep me in line. At whatever cost in pride, the Black Bart account was going to lift Perkins & Tate (Public Relations) Ltd back into solvency, and I wasn't going to blow it.

Now, however, I sank into a straight chair in the wings and did my best to give an imitation of an immovable object. If Bart wanted any more errands done, he could get one of the stagehands to do them. I was off duty for the night—off active duty. I was still on entourage duty, as was Gerry, and no more pleased about it than he was. But I knew that, like me, he was visualizing the long columns of red ink in the Perkins & Tate ledgers slowly

turning black. He'd put up with a lot of inconvenience
for that result, too. It would pay for a lot of birdseed,
later.

Fortunately, the Client had been in a better mood
since we reached the theatre. The house was full, book-
ings were solid for the remainder of the engagement
and, when he glanced out through the curtains, he'd
found the first half-dozen rows filled with giggling teenage girls. He was looking almost cheerful when he went
to his dressing-room to get ready for his entrance.

Gerry had joined the crap game that was carrying on in
the Cousins' dressing-room, and was practising while they
opened the show. I could hear Sam arguing with Lou-Ann
in her dressing-room. It was the same old argument about
comedy technique. I wondered why he didn't give it up.
Lou-Ann didn't feel safe with a joke unless she hammered
it into the ground with crossed eyes and a pratfall. It was
too bad, but that was the way it was.

'Trust the lines, baby, I promise you—they're funny.
You don't have to do anything to them.' Sam followed
her out of the dressing-room, brushing at a speck of
powder on her jacket, too absorbed in her to notice me
sitting there. 'Just relax and throw them away. Try it.
Just for tonight—try it. You'll see—it will work.'

'Yes, Sam,' she said mechanically. For a moment, he
looked hopeful, as though he thought he'd got through
to her. He forgot that it was part of her nature to agree
if she thought she'd make someone happy by it. It was
another manifestation of the irresistible impulse to make
them laugh. They *had* to like her. She'd promise anything, but forget the promise the instant the spotlight
hit her. In as short a time as I'd known her, I realized

that. Sam must know it, too, but he was as incapable of relinquishing his dream as Lou-Ann was of changing the technique she believed tried and true.

'That's a good girl.' He patted her on the shoulder. 'Now, go on out there and remember what I told you.'

'All right, Sam.' She paused before her entrance, adjusted her hat to a wilder angle, and I caught the tell-tale movement of her tongue across her teeth. When she turned to smile at Sam, the liquorice gum was blacking out her two front teeth. She bounced onstage, and we heard the thump of her pratfall above the shrieking laughter of the front rows.

Sam's shoulders slumped, defeated. I nodded to him, but there didn't seem to be anything to say. He stood beside me, wincing, as Lou-Ann threw herself about with extra emphasis. She seemed to have taken Sam's pep talk as an indication that she wasn't being funny enough, and she was determined to outdo herself tonight.

'It was a nice try,' I said.

'She can't relax.' He shook his head. 'Maybe, if she just had more confidence in herself . . . But that bastard—'

I glanced at Sam, but he didn't seem to realize what he had said. Or attach any significance to it. Of course, anyone who knew Bart inevitably referred to him as 'that bastard'—but no one seemed to connect it with Maw Cooney's last words. Or was I just imagining it all? But Maw Cooney was dead—I hadn't imagined that.

'What have you heard from the police?' The thought followed naturally.

'Police?' Sam looked as blank as though I had been speaking in an unknown language.

'About the inquest,' I reminded him. 'About releasing the body.'

'Oh, that.' He withdrew his attention from the stage with an effort. 'We shouldn't have any trouble. They'll keep it as quiet as they can. Bart being a big star with a big teenage following, they're a little nervous about getting a courtroom full of fans just along for the ride. They'll probably have it in a few days, with no advance publicity, first thing in the morning, at some quiet out-of-the-way place. We don't have to worry about a thing.'

'Not even about the verdict they'll bring in?' I couldn't resist it. He was so complacent. So sure that all we had to worry about was an undignified deluge of fans.

'Verdict?' He looked at me as though I were mad. Perhaps I was. 'It was a traffic accident. You heard what the cop said—Misadventure. What other verdict could they bring in?' But he was subtly shaken. Perhaps it was the first time it had occurred to him that there might be any doubt.

Before I could answer, the Client stood in front of us. I wondered how long he had been lurking within earshot. He didn't speak, just paused long enough to rake us with an arrogant, menacing glance, then continued onstage. We could hear the audience going wild. Even backstage, the air vibrated with that haunting, hypnotic beat I was beginning to hate:

'Homesteader, Homesteader,
'Ridin' alone . . .'

Sam and I stayed silent throughout the song. Whatever his thoughts were, they must have been nearly as depressing as mine. He grew steadily gloomier.

Bart held up his hand for silence after the song ended.

He didn't seem displeased when it took longer than usual for the audience to quieten down.

'Now, folks,' he said, 'I want to introduce another little number I wrote myself—jes' like "Home-steader"—' It took another moment for the pandemonium to die down. 'Yessir, it was inspired by a wonderful little lady, who had the misfortune to be killed in a traffic accident a couple of days ago, here in your wonderful city. It sorta cast a pall on the whole Troupe, even though we're carrying on, like she woulda wanted us to. Especially—'

He went into the spiel about Lou-Ann then, and I stopped listening as I tried to control my queasy stomach. All this just-plain-folksiness was going to give me my first ulcer, if I wasn't careful. I tried not to look at Lou-Ann, smirking and taking bows.

A soft rustle behind me drew my attention. Crystal had slipped into the wings to stand watching the stage with shining eyes. "He's going to sing it now,' she murmured softly. 'Oh, it's *so* pretty.'

Well, it was nice for Bart, I supposed, to have a permanent fan club in a member of his own family. It doesn't always work that way with families. But it didn't help the state of my stomach.

'Yessir.' Bart, onstage, was returning to the main business of the evening. The spotlight snapped off Lou-Ann abruptly and was all his own again.

'Yessir, our own Maw Cooney was my inspiration for this special number I'm introducing here tonight—for the very first time anywhere!' He waved a hand, and the Cousins picked up the downbeat.

The lyrics were about as mawkish as you'd expect, but the melody was strong, wistful and haunting. And the audience was loving it. In all fairness, I'd have liked it myself if Bart hadn't been responsible for it. For a moment, I mused on the injustice of talent—why did so much of it have to be given to people one ordinarily wouldn't wish to associate with?

The song had brought Sam out of his gloom. I could see his brain cash-registering the probable sale of the record. Obviously, the next hit record for Black Bart and the Troupe. It was a spellbinder.

But, as the song continued, I was more than spell-bound—I was riveted. Something about it began to seem terribly familiar. I had heard that song—that melody—before. And not so very long ago.

''It's *so* pretty,' Crystal was murmuring in a soft litany behind me. 'Beautiful. It's jest *so* beautiful.'

Then Uncle No'ccount, who had been standing thoughtfully in the background, lifted his harmonica to his lips and joined in. The low mournful wail of the harmonica added an extra dimension to the song, breathed soul into the melody.

It also brought recognition.

Black Bart's 'Tribute to Maw' was the melody I had heard Uncle No'ccount doodling on his harmonica soon after the Troupe had arrived in London. Doodling, experimenting with, working into shape.

Black Bart might lay claim to it—but the song was no more his than Buckingham Palace. Uncle No'ccount had written it, and Bart was claiming the credit. And, if that were the case, then could Bart have written 'Homesteader', either?

'He's really got something there,' Sam said softly. 'Maybe an all-time winner. Do you realize we've never had any song for Mother's Day? Oh sure, there's

'Mother Machree', and 'M Is for the Many Things She Gave Me'—but never a 'White Christmas' kind of song the disc jockeys would keep coming back to, year after year. If we could promote this one the right way . . .' He trailed off, lost in dreams of avarice too deep for words. I didn't need to look up to know that there were dollar signs instead of tears in *his* eyes.

The song ended and the audience exploded into applause. And this was England, where we tend to take Dear Old Mother rather coolly, as a rule. In the States, with the whipped-up hysteria encouraged on all sides by the mass media, this could be a sensation. Especially on a Mothers' Day telecast.

Bart jumped into the wings between bows. He glared at us and pointed an accusing finger at Crystal. 'Don't you run away now, you hear?' he growled. 'I want to talk to you. You, boy—' he jerked his head at me—'you hang on to her, hear?'

'Okay, okay—' Sam was pushing at him—'but get out there. They're going crazy. Take another bow. Take an encore.'

Bart had never had any intention of doing anything else. The Cousins knew it, they waited with their instruments poised and began again as Bart came back onstage. Bart, his face back in the ingratiating smile, shrugged his shoulders deprecatingly at the audience, and went into his encore—a son any mother would be proud to own. At least, during the moments when he had a spotlight on him.

He took two encores and, while the applause was at its height, I felt a faint movement behind me. When I turned, Crystal had gone. It seemed to be Bart's day for having girls run out on him. And I was on the girls' side. At the same time, it occurred to me that this was the second girl I had let slip away, and Bart was going to be none too pleased about it. It might be a good idea to disappear myself.

I was too late. Bart was with us again, mopping his face with the sleeve of his shirt. ''Where is she?' he demanded.

'Perhaps she went to the Ladies' Room.' It wasn't very good, but it was the best I could think of. I was grateful that his costume wasn't the type that called for six-guns, he was looking at me as though he would have used them.

'I've had jest about enough of you, boy. I asked you where Crystal went. You let her get away, didn't you?'

'Why shouldn't I? I'm not your sister's keeper.'

'You sure ain't—you ain't man enough! Nobody is! You hear me?'

The front rows probably heard him, the way his voice was rising. The Cousins and Uncle No'ccount had filed offstage and were waiting to get past us. Obviously, no one felt like giving Bart a friendly nudge to move him out of the way. It would have been like shoving a wounded panther.

'Take it easy, Bart. Take it easy.' Sam, the human buffer, was working at his job again. 'Look, she can't have gone far. She only just left. I would have stopped her, but I was too busy applauding. You were great, Bart.'

Bart shook him off like a gadfly. He was too intent on trying to intimidate me. 'Some day, it's going to be you-and-me, boy!'

I stared back at him levelly. 'That wouldn't surprise me a bit.'

He turned abruptly, and his eye fell on the unlucky Uncle No'ccount. 'I want to talk to you, too,' he snarled. 'Come on.'

'Bart.' Lou-Ann moved in front of Uncle No'ccount. 'Bart, why don't we jest go home? I'm awful tired. Please, Bart.' She clung to his arm. 'Let's go.'

On a vague impulse to close ranks with anyone Bart was gunning for, I walked over to Uncle No'ccount. I had chosen the wrong moment, and got there just as he was putting back his teeth. I saw him catch my expression from the corner of his eye, and the flicker of amusement.

'Why the hell do you do that?' To cover my revulsion, I snapped at him. 'You can play perfectly well wearing those things. I've heard you.'

'Well, now,' he said gently. 'It was Bart's idea—his orders, sorta. After all, there can't be more than one glamour boy in the act now, can there?' Something in his voice, perhaps in the very lack of expression in his face, travestied the remark. I grinned involuntarily. If Lou-Ann could ever learn to deliver a line with that expression and that timing, Sam might be on the way to his great female comic.

After a moment, something flickered in his eyes again to answer my grin. 'Not that there was ever much chance of me giving him a run for his money,' he went on. 'I'm only jest poor old Uncle No'ccount.'

But he *had* another name—and I had heard it once. Standing there, I groped after it, and then I remembered. 'Come on, Eugene,' I said. 'I'll buy you a drink.'

They had the Client almost calmed, but it set him off again when he saw us start to walk away. 'Where the hell do you think you're going, you no-account old fool?'

Uncle No'ccount turned slowly and stared at him. 'Doug here and me is going out and have a drink,' he said slowly and clearly. 'Maybe we're even goin' to talk business a little. Maybe we'll even talk about songs.'

Unbelievably, I watched the Client deflate. There had been no menace in the quiet voice. Nothing to give the game away—they couldn't know that I had recognized the tune. Yet, Bart had given way against the veiled threat.

I decided it was going to be a very interesting drinking party. There was more to Uncle No'ccount than met the eye.

CHAPTER XII

FOR THE FIRST TIME in months, Gerry and I met over the breakfast table in the morning. That is, we collided in the cupboard that serves us as a kitchen, poured boiling water into some instant coffee, dredged some biscuits and a jar of meat paste out of an almost forgotten recess, and carried everything into the office to spread out on the desk.

Gerry burbled cheerfully, reading me snippets from the morning papers, and regaling me with his own observations about them. I didn't mind. It was sheer reflex action on his part. Birds get very narky if you don't chat them up in the morning, and I knew he was so used to this breakfast routine that he hardly noticed it was only me across the desk.

I concentrated on the meat paste, wondering how long we'd had it, and how long it could keep safely. It tasted slightly odd, but that might have been the spices, and there was a faint flavour of cardboard, which was interesting in a product which had been sealed in a glass jar. I spread more on another biscuit. With any luck, I might come down with a first-class case of food poisoning and have to be taken to hospital for a while. Say, until the Client had gone back to the States.

'Did you learn anything from Uncle No'ccount last night?' Gerry folded the paper and settled down to a business conference.

'Not much.' He'd been very cagey. There had been moments when I'd thought he was secretly laughing at me. 'He wouldn't come off the act.'

'You think it *is* an act?'

'What do you think? He wrote that song, you know, 'Tribute to Maw'. He probably wrote 'Homesteader', too.'

'He *told* you that?' Gerry was incredulous.

'He didn't tell me anything, and I didn't ask. I heard him working on the melody shortly after they arrived. It was rough, but it was the same tune. I'm sure of it.'

'But, ''Tribute to Maw''—*before* anything happened to her? Do you mean he was expecting something to happen?'

It was a thought that hadn't occurred to me, and I pushed it away firmly. It might be risky, but I was excluding Uncle No'ccount from my short list of bastards. 'No,' I said, 'I think it was just the melody he was working on. Then, when this happened, he set the words to it.'

'You mean, sort of an all-purpose dirge. In case Zeke bought it, perhaps? Then, when Maw did, instead, he just switched over to her?'

'Something like that. It's a good melody. Too good for the words. If we could introduce him to a competent lyricst—'

'You're mad!' Gerry called me back to order. 'We don't want any more to do with them than we can help. In less than a month, they'll all be back in the States—and the best of British luck to the States. Don't rock the boat.'

'You're right,' I agreed. Apart from which, the Client was claiming credit for both songs, and it could be very nasty to interfere there. Whatever agreement there was between him and Uncle No'ccount—or, rather, whatever hold they had over each other—presumably it was more or less satisfactory to both, and there was nothing to be gained by an outsider coming along to upset the apple cart.

'In a way,' Gerry said thoughtfully, 'it restores my faith in human nature to know that the Client didn't write those songs. Uncle No'ccount may not be any lily, but he's a lot more fragrant than the Client.'

The telephone rang, and we looked at each other. Neither of us made a move. It went on ringing.

'We ought to answer it,' I said, with conviction. 'It might be Penny.'

'Or Amanda,' Gerry said. 'Or Samantha, or Jane.' He got up and crossed to the phone. 'Or Christine, or Kate, or . . . Good morning. Perkins & Tate.' His face fell, and he listened without saying anything. I had already felt in my bones that it was the Client. It was going to be that kind of day—again.

'Charming,' Gerry said, replacing the phone and tottering to the kitchen for more coffee. 'We are invited to drag our arses over there just as fast as we can get the lead out.' He came back, sipping coffee, and slumped across the desk from me.

'I don't know,' he said pensively, 'perhaps I have it coming. We pay for our transgressions, and all that. But you're a reasonably clean-living chap—how did you get dragged into it?'

'Perhaps I had my fun in a previous incarnation.' I sat there hopeful, waiting for some twinge from my stomach to tell me that the meat paste was doing its deadly work. Nothing happened. I felt fine. I was fighting fit and ready to face the day—it was too bad that the day had to include the Client.

* * *

Lou-Ann opened the door to the suite. Without make-up, the circles under her eyes were blackly noticeable. She had been crying, too. It was probably unfair to blame that on the Client—after all, the girl's mother had just died. But I found myself wishing that she were still in the room downstairs.

'Come in, boys,' she said. 'It was real nice of y'all to come over here so quick-like.'

'Nice, hell!' the Client snarled. 'We're payin' them. Don't you keep forgettin' that.'

He wasn't an inspiring sight, leaning against the mantelpiece in crumpled pyjamas, unshaven and scowling. He looked more natural that way, but not very much like the Lonely Homesteader image. He might have lost a few fans, if they could have seen him like that. On the other hand, he might not. Some women like the blue-jowled brute type.

I ignored him. 'Did you get any sleep?' I asked Lou-Ann.

'Ah surely did.' She smiled wanly. 'I took one of them pills the doctor left for me. It didn't work too good, but Bart wouldn't let me take another one. I guess maybe he was right. After a while, I went to sleep. They jest take a long time to work, I guess.'

'You wanta be careful about pills.' Bart pushed himself away from the mantel and came forward. 'They ain't nothing to fool around with. I don't like you having them at all. You better give them to me.'

A nasty little chill slid down my spine. There was nothing wrong with the words, nor with Bart's expression. Even his voice was smooth and properly concerned. But it was all phoney. All too pointed.

'No.' A stubborn expression closed down over Lou-Ann's face. 'I'll keep them. I'll be all right. You don't have to worry about me none. I'm not a kid.'

With Bart, she might be better off if she were. But the offer had been made and refused now. In front of witnesses. I felt a damp perspiration break out on my forehead, and tried to convince myself that it was just the tainted meat paste taking effect. But I couldn't make myself believe it. Nothing so cheerful.

'Why don't you go lay down for a bit, honey,' Bart said, with laboured concern. 'No need for you to be up so early.'

'Maybe I will.' She smiled gratefully, but lingered. She didn't really want to exchange the life and warmth of company for a darkened room, but she was afraid of discouraging Bart by not responding enough. It was obviously the first time he had paid any attention to her since the shotgun was removed from his back.

'You git along now,' Bart urged. 'Have a little nap. You won't miss nothing. We'll all still be here when you wake up. Honest.'

'All right, Bart,' she said, and disappeared into the room, leaving the door ajar.

Bart went over and closed the door firmly, then came back to us with a worried frown. 'Ah'm really worried about that little gal,' he said confidentially. 'She is so broke up over her poor Maw that she don't hardly know what she's doing.'

I avoided Gerry's eyes, and tried to stand firm against an impulse to run screaming all the way to Scotland Yard. What could I complain about, after all? A man was telling us he was worried about his wife. It was normal, understandable, and hardly a matter for the police. But not when that man was Black Bart.

It was my imagination. It had to be. There was absolutely no evidence that Bart could be planning anything. Just as there was no evidence that Maw's death had been anything but a traffic accident. Bart was far from the most savoury client we'd ever encountered, to say the least of it. But, while molesting children might not win him the Nobel Prize, it didn't necessarily make him a candidate as a murderer, either.

'Ah know I ain't maybe been the *best* husband in the world,' he wound up with the understatement of the year. 'But I sure aim to do better by her from now on. Yessir, these past few days have showed me jest how much she really means to me.' Face alight with resolution, he turned away.

Gerry murmured something to me, but not so low that the Client didn't catch it. He whirled back. 'What did you say?' he demanded.

'Cauld grue,' Gerry replied. 'I said cauld grue didn't agree with me at this hour of the morning. It's what we had for breakfast,' he added hastily. 'You wouldn't know, it's a form of Scottish porridge.'

'Oh, too bad.' Mollified, the Client lost interest. 'Maybe you can find something for it in the bathroom. They got all kindsa things in the medicine cabinet in there.'

'That's a good idea,' Gerry said, and we both raced for the medicine cabinet. Of course, it was too simple. Bart wouldn't have been asking Lou-Ann for the pills if she'd left them in plain sight in the medicine cabinet. We went back to the living-room.

The Client had turned off the act and reverted to normal. He glared at us. 'Where the hell *is* everybody? Why ain't they here? I called them same time as I called you.'

He strode to the telephone and snatched it up. 'Try Room 437 again, will you—please?'

The door opened then, and the Cousins piled into the suite. 'Bart,' Cousin Homer whined, 'why'd you call us? Ain't we all rehearsed enough? You promised us we could take a day off and go shopping today.'

'Shut up,' Bart said, intent on the telephone. He raked them with a contemptuous glance. 'Where's No'ccount?'

Nobody met his eyes. The Cousins shuffled about unhappily. ''We dunno, Bart.' Cousin Zeke seemed to have lost some invisible toss and had to reply. 'We ain't seen him. Maybe he's gone out on one of them Tours of London.'

'Or maybe he ain't up yet.' It was impossible to place the source of the murmur. All three seemed to struggle to hold back snickers.

'Oh, there you are!' Bart's attention was diverted by the phone. 'Where the hell have you been?'

The phone crackled wildly.

'Yeah? Well, you drag it up here. Pronto!' He slammed down the receiver and swung to face the Cousins.

They weren't laughing now. They cringed across the room, trying to appear indifferent to his gaze. 'Whyn't you come with us, Bart?' Zeke offered hopefully. 'We was going over to that Harrods, they say they got everything there.'

'Naw, I can't.' Abruptly, Bart remembered his pose. 'I gotta stay here with Lou-Ann. She ain't been too good lately. I want to keep an eye on her.' His face, his voice, were suitably grave.

The Cousins obediently fell into respectful attitudes.

'Poor kid,' Cousin Homer said, in a hushed voice. 'How *is* she?'

'Restin',' Bart said. 'Leastwise, I hope so. She sure needs it. Good, normal rest, that is. She took some of them pills last night. And I don't believe that stuff does you any good at all. Worse than nothing, that stuff is.'

'It ain't so bad, Bart,' Zeke defended. 'It's right smart stuff. Ain't gonna do nobody no harm.'

I remembered now that Bart had thrown Zeke's sleeping pills overboard. Perhaps I was wronging him. Perhaps he honestly did have a 'thing' about pills, and just wanted to get rid of Lou-Ann's.

'That's what *you* say,' Bart sneered. 'I seen you eatin' them like they was candy, days you got nervous. And Lou-Ann ain't got *your* constitution. She's delicate-like.'

He might have said more, but his voice had been rising, and the bedroom door opened. Lou-Ann stood there.

'Howdy, boys,' she said. 'Nice of y'all to drop over.'

'Howdy, Lou-Ann,' they chorused, then stood abashed, as though in the presence of a skeleton at the feast. Bart was doing his work well. Already, people were less natural in her presence. That would shake her weak self-confidence even more.

A gentle tap sounded at the door of the suite. Bart frowned in that direction, but made no move. 'Answer the door,' he snapped out, to no one in particular. The Cousins collided, leaping to open it.

'Mornin', Bart. Mornin', Lou-Ann. Mornin', Boys.' Crystal slid into the room. 'Mornin'—' She turned to Gerry and me.

'Never mind the roll-call,' Bart snarled. 'Where the hell have you been?'

'Been? I ain't been nowhere,' she said defensively.

'Don't lie to me! You wasn't in your room last night. I tried to call you and the switchboard told me.'

'Yes, I was, Bart. Maybe they was ringing the wrong room.'

'Balls! And you wasn't there the night before, neither. What you playin' at?'

'Now, Bart.' Lou-Ann moved forward protectively. 'You can't tell for certain sure. Maybe that switchboard *did* make a mistake. Nobody's perfect—'

'Least of all my sister.' He grinned evilly at Lou-Ann, momentarily forgetting his concern for her. 'What's the matter—the alibi run out? Why don't you try tellin' me you been with her, playin' gin rummy the last two nights. 'Cept, this time, I *know* you ain't been. You been in here with *me* the past two nights.' He swung back to Crystal.

'What's the matter? Ain't you had time to think up another story? Or maybe you been too busy to do much thinking? Or maybe you don't even care enough to try. It ain't nothing to you that yore poor brother's worrying himself sick about you and yore future.'

'Now, Bart, that ain't so.' She was backing away slowly. 'Honest, Bart—'

'Don't you honest me.' He was advancing upon her. 'You don't know the meanin' of the word—'

'Bart, please don't, Bart.' Lou-Ann tried to halt his progress, tugging vainly at his arm. He shook her off.

The Cousins had abdicated. They huddled together a safe distance from the action. Now and again, they caught each other's eyes and a sardonic smile slid among them.

''See here, old chap.' Gerry didn't like the way things were going any more than I did. But, being a natural ladies' man, he was going to try the Galahad routine. 'Don't you think you ought—'

'You keep the hell outa this!' The Client shot him a glare that would have halted a regiment.

'Oh, well, if you feel that way about it—' Gerry retreated, as any wise man would have done.

'This is a *family* affair,' Bart said. A snicker broke from the assembled ranks of Cousins. Bart sent them a glance that silenced them, too.

'I'll tell you where you been, you little tramp,' he thundered. 'You been with *him*!'

'No, Bart, no,' she moaned. She had backed against the farther wall now, and she sidled along it. Frantically, her fingers groped behind her for escape. She was inches from one of the bedroom doors and possible safety.

'Don't lie to me!' The backhand blow caught her on the side of the head and she staggered. Her hand caught the doorknob.

'You good-for-nothin' little slut—' He raised his arm for another blow, and Lou-Ann caught at it from behind, desperately. 'You think I ain't noticed *he* ain't been around, neither? You think I'm stupid, or something?'

Crystal clawed frantically at the bedroom door and it opened. Bart knocked her through it.

'I know what you are,' he shouted. 'I been watching you. You don't fool me none.'

'Please, Bart—' Lou-Ann was still trying to calm him.

'I *know*.' Bart charged through the doorway after her. Lou-Ann followed, clutching at him. There was the sound of another vicious slap. Crystal screamed faintly.

'You an' Uncle No'ccount! You an' Uncle No'ccount! What kinda fool do you take me for? You think I don't know you go sneakin' off and sleeping with him every damn chance you get?'

The door slammed shut behind them.

I stared at the blank, forbidding door incredulously. 'Crystal and Uncle No'ccount?' I turned to the Cousins. 'He's mad, isn't he? Crystal—sleeping with Uncle No'ccount?'

Released from tension, the Cousins began to guffaw. To shuffle about, slapping each other on the back, laughing uproariously.

'Crystal—and Uncle No'ccount?' I repeated urgently, willing them to give me an answer. Although I realized the more they laughed the more I believed it. It was just the sort of thing to appeal to their sense of humour.

'Hell, boy,' Cousin Zeke finally sputtered. 'Why not? They's married, ain't they?'

'Crystal and Uncle No'ccount?' The vision came to me of Uncle No'ccount onstage, coughing his dentures into that big red bandana. A shabby, broken-down bum. 'But . . . but . . . those *teeth*!'

It was the funniest thing they had ever heard. They fell about.

In the other room, I heard Crystal sobbing.

They choked, they spluttered, they pummelled each other. They were never going to stop laughing.

'Hell, boy, why not?' Cousin Ezra gasped out. 'That's *all* he got missing!'

CHAPTER XIII

二

I WAS STILL pretty browned off when Sam come round to the office late that afternoon. 'You might have let me know,' I said. 'I'm tired of being made to feel a fool. If there's anything else I ought to know . . .'

'How much else do you think there *could* be?' Sam sank into a chair and slumped forward, arms on desk, chin on arms. 'If there there's anything else, *I* don't want to know it, either.'

'But I can't understand it. What in hell is Bart so upset about if his sister is married to the man?'

'Don't ask me,' Sam sighed. 'I only majored in business science, not abnormal psychology. Sometimes I wish I'd taken that offer from IBM—*they* can't have problems like this.'

'Perhaps it isn't too late,' I said wistfully, thinking of Cinecittà, and the warm, honest decent emotion of a fist shaken under your nose. 'Perhaps we could *all* write the whole thing off and start over again.'

'Not with a million dollars tied up already,' Sam said. 'And that's just for openers.' He glanced at me obliquely. 'I don't like to upset you, but the Agency wants to film the pilot and first couple of shows over here—production costs are a lot lower.'

The expression on my face must have given him pause. There was a short silence, during which I didn't look at him. 'I've already arranged for the pilot film to be shot tomorrow,' he said tentatively. 'We may be here an extra month.'

'My cup runneth over.'

'An extra month—can that kill you?' He was being awfully good about it, he hadn't mentioned how far the extra money would go towards turning Perkins & Tate into a profit-making organization. He didn't hit below the belt. I wasn't so delicate.

'Perhaps not—but it might kill someone else.'

'Zeke? He's over that foolishness now. He isn't scaring himself into seizures any more. An extra month won't bother him.'

'What about Lou-Ann?'

'Yeah, Lou-Ann.' Sam's face shadowed. 'She hasn't said anything, but I know she wants to get out of here. Well, you can't blame her. It's a nice town, but it hasn't exactly provided happy memories for her. On the other hand, it will be rough for her wherever she is. It takes time to get over something like that. She might as well be here as anywhere else. Besides—' He broke off sharply.

'Besides—what?' But a glimmering was beginning to get through to me. 'Haven't they quashed that indictment yet?'

'It's taking a little longer than they expected,' Sam said unhappily. 'But don't worry, they'll do it. There's too much at stake to let one stubborn old man and his jail-bait kid gum up the works. They're going to offer him more money. You'll see, he'll accept the offer.'

I turned away. There might be more at stake than

Sam realized. Should I say anything? Would he believe me, or would he continue to play the Company Man and perhaps threaten me with a slander suit? Or at least recommend removing—if not the account—then Perkins, from Perkins & Tate?

Crossing to the window, I opened it and leaned out. The weather was still holding and a crisp breeze was blowing up from the Thames. More leaves fell from the trees and blew through Embankment Gardens with each gust. Leaning just a little farther out, I caught a glimpse of Penny crossing Villiers Street, coming to work. Speaking of things at stake, that decided me.

I ducked back into the room and closed the window. 'Sam,' I said, firmly, 'I think you ought to know—'

There was a tap at the door; it opened, and I lost Sam's attention. Lou-Ann and Crystal came into the room. 'I reckoned we'd find you here, Sam,' Lou-Ann said. 'We wanta talk to you.'

'Come in. Sit down.' Sam leaped up, pushing his chair forward for Lou-Ann.

But it was Crystal who looked as though she needed to sit down. Although she had been carefully made up, she was deathly pale, and the foundation and powder didn't quite conceal the ugly bruises on her face. With a wan smile, she slumped into the chair I offered.

'Sam, you jest gotta do something for Crystal,' Lou-Ann said. 'She can't keep goin' on this way. You gotta make Bart see reason. I've tried—and I can't do nothin' with him, so it's up to you. You'll have to threaten him—or something.'

'Threaten him—with what?' Over Lou-Ann's head, Sam met my eyes and shook his head. Fine. So she didn't even know about the incident they were trying to quash back in the States. They had kept it from her.

'I don't know,' Lou-Ann said wildly. 'Threaten you'll tear up his contract, or something. But you gotta make him leave Crystal alone. It ain't even human—the way he carries on. Why shouldn't she live with her lawful-wedded husband?'

'Sam can't do nothin',' Crystal said softly. 'Bart's always been like that. I guess maybe Eugene is right. Guess maybe him and me oughta jest slide away some place where Bart can't never find us, and live in peace.'

'Now, wait a minute,' Sam said. 'You don't want to do a thing like that. Think what it would do to the act. I'll talk to Bart. Reason with him—'

'No such thing as reasoning with Bart,' Crystal said. 'Never has been—not even when he was jest a little kid. There's something in him so pig-headed mule-stubborn, he don't even know other people are alive—'less he happens to need them. I guess maybe he's kind of crazy.'

'Don't say that!' Sam was anguished, perhaps because the same thought had occurred to him at times. 'Bart's just very high-strung, that's all. He's a very talented boy and he lives on his nerves, like a lot of talented people.'

'That's true,' Lou-Ann said softly. 'Bart is very sensitive. So many people don't realize that.'

The difference was that Lou-Ann believed it. Sam was just trying to protect the Agency investment. He couldn't fool Crystal, though. She had known Bart longer than either of them. She looked as unconvinced as I felt.

'Look at it this way,' Sam pleaded. 'It's only for a

few more weeks. You've gone this long. Why call a halt now?'

'He never hit me before,' Crystal said. 'He's getting worse.'

The door opened and Penny came in, hesitating as she saw the office full of people. Sam glanced at her wildly, as though trying to assess her value as a possible ally, then dragged her into the argument.

'Think of the fans,' he said. 'Think of all those trusting kids who'll be disappointed if Bart gets so upset he cancels the engagement. Look, here's the President of the Fan Club. Just ask her how she'd feel if he gave it all up.'

'I'd be delighted,' Penny said. She noticed that Lou-Ann was there, and blushed, but didn't retreat. 'I'm sorry,' she said, 'but I think he's perfectly frightful.'

'Okay,' Sam said, 'okay.' He pulled a fiver out of his pocket and threw it at her. 'Run and get us four coffees, will you? Get one for yourself, if you want. Just hurry!' Penny caught the money and vanished.

'I don't want any coffee.' Crystal tried to stand up, but Sam pushed her back into her chair.

'Calm down,' he said, although she was a lot calmer than he was. 'Think of what you're doing. It's not just Bart—it's all of you. You're on the threshold of the Big Time now. On the way up—real UP. What you've had so far is just a drop in the bucket, compared with what you could have a year from now. Just as long as you don't make waves.'

'That's all nothing to do with me,' Crystal said. 'I'm not in the act. It can go on without me bein' around and wouldn't make no never-mind to nobody.'

Except to Bart. Who had already hinted at plans to

bring Crystal into the act. And that was a disturbing thought I didn't care to examine. There wasn't really room for more than one female in the Troupe.

'But you said No'ccount would go with you. That would cut into the Troupe. I mean, he's a nice character-piece, sort of an anchor to hold down the whole thing.' With a nervous look at me, Sam tried to telegraph his meaning to Crystal. 'It would upset Bart if he left, too.'

'I expect it would,' Crystal smiled.

'Of course,' Sam covered quickly, 'I suppose it wouldn't make all that much difference. Bart's the one the customers pay to see. He's got the voice, the presence, the talent—'

'Not all that much talent.' I could keep quiet no longer. 'He didn't write those songs.'

'How do you know?' Sam choked, taken off guard.

' "Tribute to Maw" ,' I said. 'I heard Unc—' I caught myself. Even more than Uncle No'ccount, his wife must be yearning for his proper identity. The identity Bart, for reasons of his own, had stripped from him. I tried again.

'I heard Eugene working on it in its early stages. It's a very haunting tune. Naturally, I recognized it when it went into the act.'

'Then you *do* know,' Crystal said gratefully.

'He wrote "Homesteader", too, didn't he?'

'Of course,' she said. 'You don't think Bart did, do you?'

'Wait a minute, wait a minute,' Sam said. 'Now, it's lucky we're all family here, so to speak. But remember, the arrangement was that Bart was going to take the credit for those songs.' He smiled cravenly at me.

'You understand these things,' he said, 'It's just the

publicity platform. It makes a stronger story if Bart
writes his own material. It gives him more depth. It's
in the Tradition.'

I nodded, just to tell him that I was registering what
he said, not that I approved of it. There was a lot I
could have said, but I found myself inhibited by Lou-
Ann's presence. She had been quiet during the discussion, so I gathered that this was one of the few secrets
she *was* privy to.

'You needn't worry,' Sam said. 'It's all open and
above-board in the contracts. Uncle No'ccount is collecting the royalties on any songs he writes. So, what
does it matter where the credit goes? He's going to be
rolling in the green stuff in a few more years—if he
keeps turning them out. What more could he want?'

'Nothing,' I said. 'Except, perhaps, the chance to put
his teeth in, once in a while.'

Lou-Ann turned away. I wondered how much she admitted to herself of insight into Bart. How much could
she admit and still remain sane? But her presence certainly put a damper on the discussion.

'That's just part of the routine,' Sam argued. 'It's
establishing a character. He stands out in a crowd because of that. There's nothing wrong with—'

'It turns him into a buffoon,' I said. 'It hides the fact
that *he's* the one with the talent. All the Client has is a
set of sexy pipes. Perhaps, if the public caught on to
that, they might start paying attention to Eugene, who
has a lot more to recommend him.'

'Oh yes,' Crystal breathed. 'You *do* understand. You
do see! There's jest so much music in him that everything sings when he's around. There's a kinda magic in
the whole world when he's standing beside you, looking

at it with you. Everything is brighter, and cleaner, and softer, and *better*.'

Lou-Ann sobbed suddenly. Just once.

Sam was beside her instantly. 'Come on,' he said, 'let's get out of here.' He pulled her gently to her feet and led her from the room, while she was still scrabbling frantically in her handbag for a Kleenex.

'It's too bad.' Crystal looked after them, shaking her head. 'Bart is jest plain no-good, and that's the truth of it. I could of told them that. Her Maw should never have let it happen, instead of encouraging him all the time. It was all right for *her*, but he's been taking it out on Lou-Ann ever since.'

Perhaps, finally, he had taken it out on Maw herself. But it was not a thought to voice to his sister, even though she didn't seem to be a member of the Fan Club, either.

'Lou-Ann, she won't ever learn now,' Crystal went on, analysing her sister-in-law. 'Maybe she don't even want to. Bart, he was jest about the biggest, most exciting thing that ever happened to her. And,' she added thoughtfully, 'he was 'bout the only thing she ever truly wanted that her Maw let her have.'

I began to feel that the right person had been killed, but for the wrong reason. Any reason Bart could have had *must* have been wrong. He wasn't doing anyone any favours—least of all his wife.

I had forgotten the coffee. Penny opened the door and staggered through, precariously balancing five cups of coffee in a cardboard box that was beginning to buckle in the middle. I hurried forward and rescued the makeshift tray.

'Where is everybody?' she asked.

'Now, Bart.' Penny's question had obviously raised an echo of Bart's cry in Crystal's mind, too. 'You take Bart,' she continued, ignoring the fact that anyone who had known him for half an hour wouldn't have had him as a gift.

'Bart, he thinks he's king of the castle—everybody's castle. He ain't learned yet that there's things he can't do. Why, do you know?'—an amused smile curved her lips—'he still thinks he can split up Eugene and me.'

'Amazing!' I said. 'Here, have a cup of coffee. Drink up. We have two apiece.'

'Yessir.' She accepted the coffee and sipped at it thoughtfully. 'He was glad enough to have me marry Eugene when he was jes' starting out and needed some good material. There are plenty of singers around, you know. But if they ain't got the real good songs to sing, they're nothin'. And that's what Bart was—nothing. Until Eugene started writing songs for him.'

Penny was quietly drinking her coffee in the corner by the filing cabinet. I knew that she was also drinking in every word. It was all right—I trusted her to be discreet, but I couldn't help thinking how upset Sam would be, if he knew. He had sent her out for coffee precisely to keep her from learning these little trade secrets.

'Now Bart's ridin' high—and he thinks I oughta do better for myself.' She glared at me suddenly, as though I might challenge the statement. 'There ain't no better!'

'I'm sure of it,' I said. Perhaps I was the only one to hear the footsteps coming up the stairs. Even though I raised my voice slightly, I meant what I said. 'His songs are brilliant. The more I learn about your Eugene, the more I admire him. I only wish I'd had the chance to get to know him properly.'

'Thank you.' He was in the doorway, then. 'I take that mighty kindly.'

'Eugene!' Crystal dashed forward and hurled herself into his arms.

'All right, honey.' He hugged her, then held her away from him, frowning, as he studied her bruises. 'We're finished,' he said. 'We get us out from under, as of right now. I found us a little flat, like they say here, and we move in today. It don't matter what Bart says—I'm not having you near him any more. I shoulda done this long ago.'

Crystal didn't hesitate. 'All right, Eugene,' she said.

'You tell Bart—' Eugene Hatfield glared at me fiercely over his wife's shoulder—'this is the end of the road. If he still wants me in the act—okay. If he doesn't—that's okay, too. But Crystal and I are moving out. No more separate hotels, no more scenes, no more being split up. You tell him that.'

'I'll try,' I said. In ancient times, messengers had been slaughtered for bearing less unwelcome messages. 'Do you mind if I break it to him gently?'

'Do it any way you like, boy,' Eugene said. 'Just make sure it's loud and clear. We don't want him bothering us any more. We've had it. We're on our own now.'

'Fine,' I said. 'Congratulations. Count on me for a silver fish slice—or something.'

He smiled at me. He looked taller now, more self-assured. It was a phenomenon I had noticed before. With his teeth in, and Crystal by his side, perhaps he could stay that way. If Bart could be kept from interfering.

'You know,' he said conversationally, 'once upon a

time, I actually took a degree in music. Oh, not in any college you'd recognize, I expect. Just some cornpone little place that called itself an Institute of Learning. But it was a genuine degree.' He grinned. 'Maybe, someday, I'll compose a symphony.'

'I'd like to hear it,' I said.

'Maybe you will.' He grinned again, turned, then hesitated and turned back.

'Meanwhile,' he said, 'like they say, *"Mention my name in Cheboygan—but don't tell them where I am."* '

Then they were gone.

But I had received the message. I wouldn't tell Bart where they were. For one thing, I couldn't. They hadn't told me where they were going.

CHAPTER XIV

NOT BEING ANXIOUS to deliver the message about Crystal, I found it easy to develop a guilt complex about neglecting our other clients. True, they weren't very well paying, but they might be some day. And a little more publicity might help them towards that happy time. I spent the rest of the day working on their behalf.

In any case, Uncle No'ccount had given me permission to break the news gently to Bart. If I stayed away long enough, it might seep through to him by osmosis. You couldn't get gentler than that.

The telephone began to ring in the cold grey light just before dawn. After lying there for a few moments, thinking of the things I'd say if it turned out to be a wrong number, I dragged myself out of bed.

But a telephone ringing in the night has an urgency all its own. I nearly collided with Gerry, who had also put on a last-minute spurt to answer it.

'Makes you long for the good old days when we were disconnected for lack of payment, doesn't it?' Gerry asked, picking up the receiver.

'Now see here,' he said firmly. 'Suzette moved eighteen months ago. I do wish you'd try to spread the word.

We're tired of you and the rest of her friends. This is a respectable business establishment these days.'

The voice on the other end of the line was terse and loud. I had no trouble hearing the words.

'Get over here,' Sam said. 'Quick. Lou-Ann took too many pills.'

'She shouldn't of done it,' Bart moaned, pacing the room like a caged panther. 'She shouldn't of done it.'

Sam appeared briefly in the bedroom doorway, looking haggard and harassed. 'The doctor's with her,' he said. 'She'll pull through—if there aren't any complications.'

'Complications!' Bart swung on him, gripping his shirt front and pulling Sam to him. 'What do you mean—complications?' It was a good act, but he was overdoing it.

'How do I know? Do I look like a doctor?' Eyeing Bart with cold loathing, Sam detached himself from Bart's grasp. 'How did this happen, anyway? I thought you were supposed to be looking after her.'

'I can't watch her *every* little minute!' Bart flung his arms out wildly. 'I told her to give me those pills. I never wanted her to have them at all. She was jest too wrought-up. Accounta her Maw an' all. An' she was even worse yesterday—because we was gonna shoot the pilot tomorrow. I mean, today.'

Gerry and I were watching him nearly as coldly as Sam. Bart obviously felt his audience wasn't with him. 'Doc! Doc!' He lurched brokenly towards the doorway, seeking more receptive material. 'Doc, how is she?'

'I'll speak to you later.' The doctor closed the door

firmly in his face. It looked as though we had yet another resignation from the Fan Club.

'Shouldn't we be doing something?' Bart wheeled back towards us. 'Ain't there *nothin'* we can do?' He flicked a snakelike glance at me. 'We sure could use that little gal o' yours now—to go an' fetch us some coffee.'

'What's the matter with Room Service?' I asked.

'They've sent coffee up once,' Sam said hastily. 'We don't want them to pay too much attention to what's going on here. We don't want any publicity about this.'

'Hell, no!' That was at least one point on which Bart and Sam agreed. 'That's what I said—we sure could use that little gal o' yours right now.'

'She doesn't work after five o'clock,' Gerry said. 'She's only a kid, you know.' I saw him remember, too late, that that was Penny's main virtue in Bart's estimation.

'Who discovered what had happened?' I asked.

'I came by,' Sam said, 'to talk over a few points before we started filming the pilot tomorrow . . .'

'It's today now,' Bart put in. 'I sure hope Lou-Ann will be able to make it. What a terrible, terrible thing to happen right just now.'

I bit back the impulse to ask him when he would have liked it to happen. Gerry and I exchanged glances, then crossed to the sofa and sat down. Sam and Bart might be willing to spend the rest of the night on their feet, pacing about; but, with all due respect to the lady, Gerry and I were not so involved with Lou-Ann as they were.

'I wanted to talk to Lou-Ann, too.' Sam turned to face us. 'So we knocked on her bedroom door. And when we couldn't rouse her—'

'I went in,' Bart declared. 'I'da broke the door down, if I'd had to.' He seemed to wait for applause that didn't come, then went on quickly. 'I went in. She was sleepin' jest like a baby, 'cept she wouldn't wake up. So, Sam here—'

'Our Hero tiptoed out,' Sam said bitterly, 'telling me we shouldn't disturb her. I looked in, and called the doctor quick.'

'*I* was gonna call the doctor,' Bart said indignantly. 'You jest didn't give me a chance. I called everybody else, didn't I?'

'You always do,' Sam said.

The doorbell shrilled sharply. Bart leaped to answer it. 'Shhh,' he said, as the Cousins filed into the room. At their best, presuming I had ever seen them in that state, they had always seemed almost a subhuman species. Now, blue-jowled, narrow-eyed and grunting, they were pure Neanderthal, ready to crouch beside a flickering watchfire and gnaw the raw meat off some dinosaur bones before going out to bash a few heads in.

To Bart, they were a welcome audience, however. Hardly pausing to close the door, he launched into his act. 'Boys, it's jest terrible,' he said. 'You won't hardly believe this. Our poor little Lou-Ann has took an overdose of them sleeping pills.'

Cousin Zeke yawned hugely. 'Too bad,' he said, after waggling his jaw to make sure he hadn't dislocated it.

'Well, we all gotta go *some* way,' Cousin Ezra said.

'She was a real nice gal.' Cousin Homer tried for a more human touch. 'We're sure gonna miss her.'

'Miss her?' Bart demanded indignantly. 'What the hell you talkin' about? She ain't dead.'

'If she ain't,' Cousin Ezra said, 'then why'd you drag us all over here?'

It was a fair question, but it seemed to infuriate Bart. 'Because, God damn it!—I thought you'd want to know.'

'Sure we do, Bart,' Cousin Homer said. 'But morning woulda been time enough. Seeing as nothing really happened. We didn't get to bed till late, what with rehearsing for tomorrow, and all.'

'It's today!' Bart snapped. 'Today! And she plays this damfool trick. Now, what are we gonna do?'

'Postpone it?' Cousin Zeke suggested helpfully.

'Hell, no!' Bart shot him a murderous glance. 'You think our little Lou-Ann would want *that*? She's a Trouper—like her Maw before her. The one thing they always said to me was, "The Show must go on." An' that's jest what we're gonna do—go on. It's only the first show we're filming today. Won't make no difference if she misses that.' He glanced sideways at Sam. 'Like, maybe we can mention her a coupla times—give her a big build-up, so next show she comes on and there's an audience all waiting for her.'

Reluctantly, Sam nodded. 'The studio is booked, all the technicians will be there, we're on a tight budget. If she can't make it, I'm afraid that's what we'll have to do. We might be able to cut her scenes in later.'

'Why, shore, it's only plain old common hoss sense,' Bart agreed. He shrugged deprecatingly, but there was a glint of satisfaction deep in his eyes.

I rose to my feet, abruptly and instinctively. Then felt immediately foolish. There was nothing I could challenge him on. So, I didn't like the look in his eye. You can't hang a man for the look in his eye. It jest plain isn't evidence.

Bart looked at me expectantly. 'Er . . . I thought I'd see how Lou-Ann is coming along,' I said lamely.

'Me too.' He moved towards the bedroom doorway with me. 'I sure am worried about that little gal.'

I thought it would serve him right if I were sick on the carpet and the cost of taking it up and cleaning it were added to his bill. But a lifetime of training as an English gentleman prevailed, and I smiled weakly and let him accompany me.

He stalked up to the bedroom door, threw it open, then hesitated. 'You better ask,' he said, evidently remembering the doctor's treatment of him.

I looked in. Lou-Ann was sitting up, wrapped in a blanket. She lifted her head and smiled wanly at the sound of Bart's voice, but the doctor hurried across to the door and shut it again. He didn't both to say anything. He didn't need to. The one exasperated look he gave us was enough.

'I think we'd just be in the way in there,' I said.

Bart shrugged. He peeled off and began circling the room in a smooth, loping stride, like a jungle cat pacing its cage. I sat down, but couldn't keep my eyes away from him. Neither could the others.

The sky was lightening outside. The Cousins slumped in chairs, yawning and semi-comatose. Sam chain-smoked, standing by the fireplace. Gerry leaned back against the cushions, his eyes half closed. But we were all watching Bart. It was like the black hush before a storm broke with ferocity.

Meanwhile, I had a slight brainstorm of my own breaking. It had something to do with Bart's insistence that the show must go on—without Lou-Ann—and something to do with a crack Bart had made a few days ago, which had sunk to the bottom of my subconscious without fully registering. He'd snarled something about Sam's having thought the show could go on without anyone *but* Lou-Ann.

But Sam had never told Bart that, he'd have done everything in his power to keep Bart from suspecting he'd been slated to be dumped. Sam had told *me*, however. And I, like a fool, had told Maw Cooney. Maw, who could have qualified for one of the original members of Blackmail, Incorporated. Very shortly afterwards, Maw was dead. And now, Lou-Ann had taken an overdose.

But there was still no evidence.

Bart stopped pacing abruptly. The effect was like a clap of thunder. We all sat up straight. Bart glared around the room menacingly.

'Where *is* everybody?' he demanded.

I discovered I was going to enjoy this, after all. I sat back and waited.

The Cousins looked blank. Or blanker than usual. Sam lit a cigarette from the stub of another, pausing only to gnaw at a fingernail he suspected of growing. It must be unnerving to be solely responsible for steering a potential several-million-dollars-worth of gelignite. And the road was getting bumpy.

'Come on,' Bart snarled at them. 'Come on—where is she? Where's Crystal? And where's Uncle No-'ccount?'

'We don't know, Bart,' Cousin Homer said placatingly. 'We thought they must be with you. They most always are.'

'Well, they ain't. You can see that, can't you? Now, where the hell are they?'

'Maybe they're on the way,' Sam suggested. 'It isn't easy to find a taxi at this hour of the night—morning.'

'And maybe they ain't comin' at all,' Bart snarled.

Sam's eyes appealed to me to say something helpful. Bart intercepted the signal and whirled on me. 'What do *you* know about this?'

'As a matter of fact,' I said, 'I don't believe they *are* coming.'

'You don't believe they *are* coming,' he mimicked me. 'Why don't you believe it, boy?' He advanced on me menacingly. 'You better tell me now, 'cause I intend to *know*.'

'Eugene sent a message,' I *was* enjoying this. Whether I would continue to do so depended on how much nearer Bart came, and what he would do when I gave him the message.

'Well?' he said. 'I'm listening.'

'Eugene found a flat. He and his wife have moved in. He said they're tired of . . . living in hotels.'

'He did, did he?' Bart's eyes narrowed dangerously; he was a tiger about to pounce. 'An' what does he think he's gonna do for a job? How's he gonna support her, like I done all these years?'

'He realizes he may be out of the act,' I said. 'I don't believe it matters very much to him. In any case—' it was another dart in the side of a wounded jungle cat— 'he'll do quite well from his royalties from all those songs, won't he?'

'You know, boy—' the eyes were slits now—'I could do real good without you.'

Sam moved forward nervously. 'Now, now, we don't want to be too hasty. I mean, we're already going to be one short, shooting the pilot—we can't have Uncle

No'ccount missing, too. We can sort these difficulties out later.' He appealed to Bart desperately. 'The Show Must Go On.'

'Yeah,' Bart said thoughtfully. 'Yeah.'

'This is no time for temperament,' Sam went on. 'Let's bury the hatchet.'

'Yeah.' Bart smiled at me, leaving me in no doubt where he would like to bury it. 'Sam's right, boy. You tell Uncle No'ccount to be on hand, jest like usual. We'll get this pilot film done first, then we'll take care of the other details.'

'I'll tell him.' I had no intention of admitting that I didn't know where he was, or how to reach him. 'But I can't guarantee that he'll show up. He was rather upset. He didn't like seeing his wife bruised.'

There was no doubt at all. I must never stand at the top of a flight of stairs, or walk down a dark alley, with Bart behind me.

'You jest *get* him here, boy,' he said softly.

CHAPTER XV

THE PHONE was ringing when we returned to the flat later that morning. A voice began without preliminary when I picked up the receiver.

'How'd he take it?'

'He managed to refrain from chewing the carpet,' I said. 'But then, there were quite a few witnesses.'

'Crystal has been pretty worried,' he said drily, 'but I promised her Bart would survive.'

'That's more than might be said for some of the others,' I told him. 'We've been there most of the night. Lou-Ann took an overdose of sleeping pills.'

I knew we were still connected, I could hear him breathing. After the silence had gone on for quite a while, I said tentatively, 'Hello . . . hello . . . ?'

'I'm still here,' he said slowly. 'You see now why I wanted Crystal out of there?'

'Then I haven't been imagining anything. You think so, too.'

'I don't think nothin'.' The voice was instantly guarded and retreated into the uneducated vernacular. ' 'Tain't up to me to do no thinking. All I called for— I was jest wonderin'—do I still have a job?'

'You've still got a job,' I told him, 'but don't try any

heroics—like turning your back on Bart if he's got a knife in his hands.'

'Don't worry, my mother done trained me never to accept no candy from strange men. An' he's about as strange as they come . . .' Again, there was silence, punctuated only by breathing. Then: 'Lou-Ann, is she . . . ?'

'They got her in time,' I said. 'Sam went up to the suite to check over a couple of points in the script. He called a doctor. They may have to write her out of the opening script, but she ought to be able to appear in the next one.'

'I see . . .'

Perhaps he did, but I hammered it home. 'That's why Bart has declared a truce over you. If the ranks get too decimated, the Public is likely to notice it.'

'Or the Agency,' he said, his voice crisp again.

'It wouldn't look too well for both you and Lou-Ann to be missing, so Bart is expecting you at the Studio at 2.00 p.m. They're planning to work right through until the show is in the can—regardless of the overtime. The Agency can stand it.'

'You gonna be there, too?'

'We'll all be there,' I promised him. 'The entire staff of Perkins & Tate, what's left of the Troupe, plus assorted cameramen, lighting experts, technicians, et cetera. You'll be surrounded by well-wishers and—more important—witnesses. It ought to be safe enough.'

'I wasn't thinking of that,' he said cryptically. 'I'll be talking to you there.' He rang off.

At first, I thought they were joking. Because it hadn't been part of the original plan to film in this country,

Sam must have had to settle for whatever studio he could find. It looked like an overgrown gardening shed at the bottom of a suburban garden. But inside, picking our way through the cross-hatching of lighting cables along the floor, it was fitted out nearly as professionally as one might wish. In the old days—seven or eight years ago—almost every shed had harboured a Group, recording demonstration records, hoping to hit the Big Time. These days, every ambitious lad who could focus a camera was filming pilots or documentaries—still hoping for the Big Time.

Except that Black Bart and the Troupe had it made already. Their shows were sold, and filming was a formality. There were a few hungry-looking individuals sitting along the walls, eagerly watching the proceedings. Evidently the original inhabitants of the studio, who had subleased to Sam, retaining visiting privileges in the hope of learning something, or meeting someone. The usual bored technicians, tootling about their business, were the same all over the world.

'Hot in here, isn't it?' Penny, festooned with her protective armour of flashbulbs, picked her way gingerly among the cables.

'It's all the lights. It will get hotter before filming is over for the day.' I had no idea how prophetic I was being. I spotted Gerry over by No. 1 camera, waved, and we began making our way over to him.

We didn't get far. An arm descended around my shoulders with unpleasant familiarity. 'Well, now,' Black Bart said, 'ain't this great? And you brought the little gal along to run our errands, I see. That was real smart of you, boy.' Penny writhed uncomfortably beneath his other arm.

I wasn't cut out by nature to be a pimp. If I'd ever had any doubt of that, my revulsion now would have set me straight. Penny was here because Perkins & Tate might need her—besides which, she had pleaded to come because she had never seen a television show being filmed. It had seemed safe enough—I had assumed that the Client would be too busy to bother with her today. I had reckoned without the enormous arrogance of the man. The world was his oyster, and he was eternally poised with lemon juice and spearing fork.

Gerry spotted us and started towards us. Before he could reach us, the outer door opened and something happened behind us. Across the room, people looked our way, and beyond us. I saw the Cousins grin and nudge each other. Nothing good could have happened, I knew then, they were enjoying the situation too much.

The Client may not have been sensitive to some atmospheres, but he could tell when a storm was brewing. He removed his arm from my shoulders and, more slowly, the other arm from around Penny. He swung about slowly to face the door, and I turned with him.

Lou-Ann moved into the studio, Sam trailing proudly behind her. 'She made it, after all, folks,' he said. 'So we can go back to the original script. She's a real Trouper.'

Bart murmured his own opinion of what she was, under his breath. It was a syllable too short for 'Trouper'.

'I couldn't let you down, Bart.' Lou-Ann came up to him trustingly. 'I'm sure awful sorry for what happened. I jest can't understand it, but it was some kinda accident. Honest, it was. I never would do a thing like that to you.'

With everyone watching the scene, Bart slipped into his role. 'Don't you worry your pretty head about it, honey.' His arm snaked around her shoulders with somewhat less enthusiasm than it had encircled Penny's. ' 'Course I knowed it was an accident. You was overtired, an' forgot you'd already had your pill. That's how these things happen.'

'No, Bart.' Lou-Ann's forehead creased. 'I only took *one* pill. Honest, I did.'

'You forgot, that's all.' He gave her a shake that wasn't so gentle as it might have looked from the distance. 'You forgot,' he said again.

'Maybe you're right, Bart.' She smiled shakily, eager for his approval. 'Maybe I did forget.'

' 'Course you did.' He beamed down at her fiercely. 'It happens all the time. I'll jest have to take better care of you from now on.'

'You do that, Bart.' Her smile was stronger now. She didn't notice Sam's expression, and I wished I hadn't.

The outer door opened again, and Crystal came in with Uncle No'ccount. Bart shot them a nasty look. 'Well, well,' he said, 'the gang's all here.'

'Howdy, Bart.' Uncle No'ccount sidled past uncomfortably. Crystal walked by without speaking. The bruises were still visible beneath her make-up.

'Don't take some folks long to get high-and-mighty on a little bit of success.' Bart looked after them darkly. 'They better be pretty careful.' He raised his voice to follow them. 'They could be ridin' for one damn' big fall!'

While Bart's attention was distracted, Penny had taken the opportunity to slip away with Gerry. They took up a position on the far side of the studio, and Gerry made motions towards loading his camera.

'I'll learn 'em.' Bart turned back to me now, and his eyes narrowed. 'Maybe I'll learn you something, too, boy,' he said. 'I don't go for that lah-di-dah talking—and ain't that jest the *cutest* little old striped tie.' He flicked a finger under my tie and pulled it out of my waistcoat.

'Easy, Bart.' Sam stepped forward nervously. He needn't have worried. I wasn't going to let myself be edged into a fight. Every time Black Bart exhaled, the fumes of bourbon almost sent me reeling. He was nearly drunk, and nasty with it. We'd be lucky if he managed to finish the day's filming successfully.

'Bart.' Lou-Ann put her hand on his arm. 'Bart, I'm still kinda weak. Can't you find me a chair, so's I can sit down?'

He would rather find her a coffin. The unguarded look of pure hate that flashed across his face said so. But he was instantly in control of himself again, and the genial husband once more.

'Why, sure, we'll find you a chair, honey. Boy,' he snarled to me, 'get her a chair!'

Sam had already moved away and taken possession of one of the chairs along the wall. He brought it back and set it down behind Lou-Ann.

She sank into it gratefully and looked up, past Sam. 'Thank you, Bart,' she said.

The director called Bart on to the floor for a run-through of his first song. The Cousins were already out there, tuning up their instruments. After Bart took up his position, Uncle No'ccount ambled out to join them. Perhaps because it was just a rehearsal, or perhaps as an act of defiance, he left his teeth in throughout the number. It didn't escape Bart, he was frowning heavily as the number ended.

Lou-Ann applauded softly from behind the cameras, which seemed only to increase Bart's bad mood. Sam leaned over her chair and murmured something to her. I was standing too far back to catch it. But then, I'd been taught at an early age that three could be a crowd— an elementary fact which Sam didn't seem to have grasped yet.

The director held a brief conference with the lighting and camera men, then signalled for a take. Bart and the Cousins regrouped themselves, leaving Uncle No-'ccount slightly to one side for better camera focus. As the Cousins took up the beat, Uncle No'ccount took the red bandana from his hip pocket, hiccoughed his teeth into it, replaced it in his pocket, and breathed achingly into his harmonica. There wasn't going to be open rebellion just yet.

It was a perfect take. The director mimed satisfaction and instructed them to carry on. He was going to shoot all the numbers at one go, then splice in the dialogue and comedy bits later. It could be a lot cheaper, if it worked, than shooting in sequence. With Bart and the Troupe all warmed up and going well, there was no reason why it shouldn't work.

During 'Tribute to Maw', Crystal crossed over to stand by Lou-Ann's chair. She bent to say something to Lou-Ann, but Lou-Ann made an abrupt brushing-away motion with both hands, and Crystal straightened, frowning.

Bart was frowning, too. He had never approved of the alliance between his sister and his wife. Now that

Crystal had defied him, he would loathe it more than ever.

Just in time, he remembered that the cameras were on him. He managed to make his expression look like part of the song and stepped back suddenly, in an unrehearsed move, jostling Uncle No'ccount roughly. It could have been an accident. It was going to look all right on film, for Bart turned quickly, grappling with Uncle No'ccount, turning it into an impromptu, affectionate-looking wrestling match for a moment.

Perhaps I was the only one to notice that, in the unrehearsed confusion, Bart managed to lift the bandana containing Uncle No'ccount's teeth from Uncle No'ccount's hip pocket and transfer it to his own pocket.

It was neatly—you might say, professionally—done. I had never inquired about Bart's early career, always feeling that I would be happier if I never knew. Now, however, I felt that a lot had been explained. It was easy to visualize Bart mixing with a Fairground crowd, jostling the fat-looking suckers. A watch here; a wallet there; perhaps a ladies' purse, for light relief. With his lazy, arrogant good looks, he would have been the perfect small-time pickpocket and confidence man. Until he found he could con more money out of the suckers' pockets by singing to them.

There was nothing I could do while Bart and the Troupe were out in front of the cameras. Perhaps there was nothing I could do anyway, but I ought to try.

I edged my way over to where Sam was standing, and tapped him on the shoulder. He shrugged me off impatiently. I tapped again.

'What the hell do you want?' Immersed in his own private problems, Sam was in no mood for politeness.

'Nothing,' I said. 'I just thought you might like to know the name of a good dentist.'

'Dentist? Are you crazy?' Sam turned and surveyed me suspiciously. 'I haven't even needed a filling for the past five yeas. What the hell would I want with a dentist?'

I nodded to the scene over his shoulder, and he whirled around just in time to get his answer.

The set of songs had ended. Just as No. 2 Camera shut off, Bart eased the bandana with the teeth out of his pocket and let it fall to the floor behind him. He wound up the song with a flourish and stamping of feet. Very carefully gauged, each stamp landed precisely on the red bandana. The noise of cracking, crunching plastic sounded through the studio in the sudden silence as the guitars ceased.

Bart made a final, vicious grinding motion with his heel before following the gaze of the others to his feet. He lifted his heel from the red bandana and shrugged. 'I always told that no'ccount old fool he was too careless with them things,' he said. 'An accident like this was bound to happen one day.'

No one answered. He grew restive under the accusing stares.

'Don't make no difference, nohow,' he said defensively. 'He don't need them for the rest of the shooting. Ain't no scene where he ever wears them.'

'You shouldn't have done it, Bart,' Uncle No'ccount said quietly.

'I done nothing!' Bart raged. 'You—' he pointed to one of the lighting technicians—'you see me do anything?'

Slightly less bored than usual, the man shook his head.

'There!' Triumphantly, he pointed to someone else. 'You?' Again a headshake. 'You? . . . You? . . .'

It made no difference. Bart might choose his witnesses, but the jury knew him too well. Before their implacable faces, he wavered to a halt, glaring in baffled indignation.

The technicians, sensing an imminent explosion and, quite rightly, wanting no part of it, hurled themselves into their own jobs—each job, by some strange coincidence, removing them from the danger area. We were left in an isolated circle, surrounded by unmanned camera equipment.

In the hiatus, Crystal crossed to Uncle No'ccount, kissed him full on the mouth, and swung to face Bart. 'It makes me no never-mind,' she said calmly. 'All you've done, Bart, is make things a little awkward temporarily for Eugene. You ain't changed nothing.'

'You lousy, rotten little tramp! After all I done for you—' Bart kicked the lumpy bandana towards them and strode off towards the oversized closet at the back that was doing duty as his dressing-room.

'Bart!' Struggling from her chair, Lou-Ann ran after him.

Sam tapped me on the shoulder. 'Excuse me, Doug,' he said humbly, 'but what did you say that dentist's name was?'

CHAPTER XVI

WHILE BART SULKED in his dressing-room, the show went on. Lou-Ann and the Cousins took the floor with the fill-in bits. All run together, it was worse than ever. The Cousins finished their part of the stint and bounded out of camera range thankfully.

Left alone, Lou-Ann hurled herself about even more wildly. She gagged, mugged, slipped, acted double-jointed, and hammered her punch lines with increasing desperation. But she was playing to the world's toughest audience. More bored than ever, the technicians went about their business, not one of them cracking a smile.

'She ought to take it easier.' Sam frowned. 'She was a pretty sick kid last night.'

I nodded. We had moved over by Bart's dressing-room, so that Sam could keep an eye on him. Sam hovered back and forth between the half-open door and a corner from which he had a clear view of the proceedings on the floor. I leaned against the wall, with a clear view of neither, but able to see far more of both than I wished.

Bart was sprawled in a chair, only his boots visible through the doorway, and had been steadily drinking from a bottle of bourbon he had taken from his make-up case. His numbers were filmed, however, and all that was left in the script was a scene or two with Lou-Ann. I wondered if he were deliberately trying to avoid those.

On the other side of the studio, the Cousins were beginning to clown around, blowing off steam in pantomimed horse-play. It was nice that *some* people felt their work was finished and could relax.

Sam flitted back to the doorway. 'Somebody ought to get him some coffee,' he said. 'We'll never get through the script today, if he can't finish the last scenes.'

'I'll go.' Penny had appeared behind us. 'They have an electric kettle in the corner. It won't take long.'

'It better not,' Sam grumbled. 'Lou-Ann's nearly done with her solo stuff. It's time Bart got ready for his cue.'

I nodded to Penny and she hurried off. In a momentary lull on the floor, we could hear the homely gurgling of the bourbon being tilted again.

'Are you sure it's a good idea?' I asked. 'I mean, do you think he's really in the mood to play any scenes with Lou-Ann?'

'It's in the script,' Sam said, as though that made it Holy Writ. 'If Lou-Ann can get out of a sickbed and come down here to go on with the show, the least Bart can do is pull himself together and go on with it, too.'

It hadn't exactly been a sickbed, but I didn't feel like arguing the point with Sam. He appeared to have an infinite capacity for ignoring the nuances of a situation. Perhaps it was a form of self-protection. He might not be able to live with himself if he admitted all he noticed. Especially, feeling the way he did about Lou-Ann.

Lou-Ann was still in the spotlight, doing her best to give herself a relapse, seizure, or whatever might result from ignoring doctor's orders too soon after being snatched back from the grave. (*Had* she deliberately taken extra pills, to attract Bart's attention?) And still, no one had laughed.

Gerry, obviously with her morale at heart, was taking pictures. It cheered her visibly every time a flashbulb went off. I wondered what possible future Sam could envisage for himself, containing her. The Great Impresario? On the other hand, all things being equal, they made a well-matched pair. She was a dab hand at not seeing anything she didn't want to see, too.

'She's trying too hard,' Sam muttered in my ear.

'Try convincing her of that.' But of course, he already had. She wasn't going to believe him. Not when Bart kept egging her on to ham it up. It never occurred to her that her darling Bart might have an ulterior motive for wanting her to fall flat on her face. Like hoping she might break her neck in the process.

But there was no evidence of that. How do you convince people without evidence? Answer: you don't. You just get written off as a petty minded malicious mischief-maker. If you don't actually get sued for libel and slander. By the time they find out you may have been right, it's too late—for them. And perhaps for you, too. There isn't likely to be much future in the Public Relations field for the PRO who has openly suggested that his Client is a murderer. It can make prospective clients very nervous. Everyone has his little quirks, and the business of a PRO is to put his client's best foot forward, and try to hide the other three cloven hooves.

The Cousins were growing noisier now. It didn't re-

ally matter. If the noise was picked up by the micro-
phones, new sound could be dubbed in later. But it was
rattling Lou-Ann considerably.

I glanced across at them and, suddenly I was considerably rattled myself.

Cousin Homer started to sit down. Cousin Ezra
whipped the chair out from under him, and danced with
glee as Cousin Homer sprawled on the floor.

'You bastard!' Cousin Homer howled.

The others laughed heartily—another of Ezra's merry
little japes. But Homer was still lying there, eyes closed,
and the laughter died away. He'd hit the floor pretty
hard, he might be hurt.

'Homer? You all right, Homer?' Cousin Ezra bent
over him uncertainly. 'I was only funning, Homer.'

Lou-Ann faltered to a stop, and turned to watch anxiously. The cameraman stopped filming.

Suddenly, Cousin Homer's hands shot up and
grabbed Ezra's shirt front, pulling him off balance and
down on top of him. 'Gotcha, you bastard!' he
shouted, enthusiastically trying to put his knee through
Ezra's stomach. They rolled about, the wrestling match
deteriorating as both of them began to shake with
laughter.

Good old Cousin Ezra—who could stay mad at him?
The licensed jester of the Troupe, with his famous practical jokes. Everybody was laughing now, even Lou-
Ann, as she turned back to the cameras and went on
with her act.

Cousin Ezra—a bastard I had overlooked. A minor
bastard, and easily overlooked in the presence of such
a major bastard as Black Bart. For that reason, perhaps,
more dangerous. Cousin Ezra—whose 'jokes' had been

know to have had serious consequences before. Serious, but not deadly—so far as we knew.

But it was the sort of thing that would be just down Cousin Ezra's street. *'That bastard pushed me!'* Not any old bastard, but a particular one. One who would think it funny to push someone out into the line of moving traffic. Give him his due—he probably intended to pull her back again before anything happened. Catch her and haul her back on the pavement, while brakes shrieked all around them, and perhaps a couple of those funny, teeny English cars bumped into each other, while drivers cursed and mopped their brows. Yes, it would be a real good joke—just the job to give everyone a good, laughable, heart-stopping scare.

But the joke had failed. Perhaps because Maw Cooney had stumbled and twisted out of his grasp. Or perhaps because he had depended too much on the reflexes of an unknown driver, and the brakes of an unknown car. Ezra came from a country where cars had to be inspected every six months to retain their Road Licence. How could he dream that the English laws were so much less demanding? It was unimaginable to a citizen of a more mobile country.

And so, the spontaneous horse-play had gone wrong. Like Ezra's other failure, when a woman had landed in hospital. But *this* woman didn't recover. He couldn't laugh that off. Nor could he admit it.

Yes, Cousin Ezra was a very good bet as that murdering bastard. But again, there was no evidence.

I saw Penny, carefully balancing a brimming cup of black coffee, moving towards me, but was so absorbed in my own brooding that the fact didn't really register. I stood aside automatically to let her enter the dressing-room, and continued brooding. Perhaps *I* could get a nice quiet job with IBM . . .

About ten seconds later I heard a muffled shriek and the crash and splash of the coffee cup hitting the floor. I charged through the doorway in time to see Penny twist away from Bart's grasp, leaving a jagged piece of her blouse in his hands.

'You keep away from me,' she gasped, 'or I'll—'

'Come on, honey, don't be like that.' He was grinning. It was obvious that he enjoyed a good unequal fight.

'Leave her alone!' I snapped.

'You again, boy?' He turned on me slowly. 'I told you—I've had enough of you. You git the hell outa here and mind your own business. *You* don't give *me* orders—get that straight.'

'Bart, cut it out!' Sam was behind me in the doorway.

Bart told us both what we could do, and returned to stalking Penny. She was panicky and edging herself into a corner. I tried to signal her to get over towards the door.

Bart caught the signal out of the corner of his eye, and half-turned towards me.

It was then that Penny snatched up the bourbon bottle and brought it down over his head. The blow should have knocked him senseless, but he merely shook his head groggily, and completed the turn until he was facing me with a nasty light in his eye.

'You hit me, boy,' he said. 'Now we are really going to tangle, and I'll teach you some manners like your momma shoulda done. If'n she hadn't'a been too busy trying to figure out who your daddy mighta been.'

Where does chivalry begin and end? It was scarcely

the moment to tell him that it was little Penny who had hit him. Not that he would have believed it, anyway. He'd been looking for an excuse to fight with me for days now. He was three inches taller than I was, and about a stone and a half heavier. All I could do was brace myself and hope that Penny's blow had weakened him.

We circled each other warily and, just as he made a sudden lunge towards me, Penny hit him again. This time he swayed visibly for a moment, then sagged to the floor between us. Penny looked a bit startled at what she had accomplished.

'Nice work,' I complimented her. 'And he certainly had it coming to him.'

'Oh, it wasn't so much that,' she said. 'I simply couldn't let him hit *you*.'

It occurred to me that Penny had all the makings of a really Faithful Old Retainer. And I must encourage her along this line. It would be a pity to lose her.

'Well—' Sam moved forward and looked down at Bart glumly—'I guess that finishes filming for today.'

'Bart! Bart, honey!' Lou-Ann hurtled through the doorway and flung herself to her knees beside him. 'What happened?'

'He slipped,' I said quickly, motioning to Penny to dispose of the cracked bourbon bottle. She nodded, and quietly replaced it under the makeshift dressing-table.

'Don't y'all jest stand there!' Lou-Ann tugged at Bart's shoulders. 'Help me pick him up and get him back to the hotel. We gotta get him a doctor. He coulda hurt himself.'

Sam ground his teeth almost audibly and stooped to lift Bart by the shoulders. Ready to show willing, I picked up his feet and we lurched forward with him, while Lou-Ann fluttered along beside him. It was a pity we didn't have any stairs to negotiate—with a little careful manœuvering, we could have managed to drop him and made it look like another of those accidents.

Gerry had gone to Penny and put his jacket around her, hiding her torn blouse. 'I'll see her home,' he said quietly to me.

'He slipped,' Lou-Ann said, as we went through the studio, 'and hit his head on the edge of the make-up table.' It was a detail I didn't remember telling her, but it fitted in very well.

I saw the Cousins grin and nudge each other, and knew they had heard the beginning of the scuffle. They'd keep quiet, though, their jobs depended on it. And it wasn't the first time they'd kept quiet about Bart.

'Reckon we'll come along.' Crystal and Uncle No'ccount joined us. 'Might be something we can do.' Her eyes were on Lou-Ann as she spoke. It was obvious that she was more worried about her sister-in-law than her brother. With a brother like that, it was understandable.

There was no signal given that I could discern but, by the time we had reached the exit, the Cousins had packed up their instruments and were following along behind us. The hired cars were waiting at the kerb, and we all piled into them.

By the time we pulled up in front of the hotel, Bart was conscious enough to go through the lobby upright, supported by Sam and me. He still wasn't bright enough to navigate on his own, or take much notice of anything, though. I wondered if Lou-Ann were right and there might be some sort of damage. But I dismissed the thought—the devil looks after his own, and it was far more likely that Bart was shamming for some purpose of his own.

We all crowded into the lift, leaving no room for anyone else. I began to see the advantages of travelling in entourage. In a curious sort of way, it provided privacy. We reached Bart's suite without being approached by anyone.

Inside, the Cousins deployed themselves around the room, leaning on the furniture and swapping meaning grins.

'Like them old musicians always say.' Cousin Zeke put down his guitar. 'When a band is goin' good, and the music is loud an' sweet an' lifting you up—why, it's the next-best thing to a woman.'

'Tell that to Bart,' Cousin Homer said. 'That ain't what *he* thinks.'

'Damn tootin',' Cousin Ezra joined in. 'Bart thinks a woman is the next-best thing—to a little girl!'

They exploded with laughter. It was obviously one of their long-standing private in-jokes. Only Uncle No'ccount wasn't laughing. He was looking unusually tight-lipped and moody, but perhaps that was the effect of being without teeth.

Lou-Ann and Crystal had gone ahead into Bart's bedroom and turned down the covers. We followed and dumped Bart on the bed with no unnecessary gentleness. He groaned and seemed to pass out again. I wasn't sure whether to believe it or not.

Lou-Ann had no doubt. 'Get the doctor,' she said wildly. 'Get that doctor up here quick. Bart's real bad.'

Crystal stared down at him with something less than

sisterly concern, and it was Sam who moved to the telephone and put in the call for the doctor.

'He can't have a doctor see him like that.'' Lou-Ann was fussing around Bart, tugging at his boots, unbuttoning his shirt. 'He gotta be undressed, so's he can be examined proper.' She looked at us hesitantly, loath to admit how much Bart would hate being undressed by herself.

'Yeah.' Sam moved again, reluctantly. 'Yeah, maybe you'd better get his pyjamas—you know where they're kept.'

'Oh, sure.' She moved away eagerly. At least she knew that much. 'Bart, now, he wouldn't like being seen in nothing but his best.' She pulled open a drawer.

'He got a real pretty pair he bought in Savannah last year.' She rummaged through the drawer—awkwardly, as she did everything. 'It's dark red, with gold dragons embroidered on it. Now, that's the sorta thing it would be good for his image for the public to see him in. Maybe you could take some pictures—' She tossed things about in the drawer frantically.

'I jest know they're here somewhere. I'm sure of it. I saw him put them there when he unpacked. Oh, here they are.' She started to pull them out of the drawer. I was watching her and saw her slowly freeze.

She stood there, the dark red pyjamas spilling like blood from her hands, and gave that funny little squawk of hers. Which wasn't really funny—especially this time.

We were all drawn across the room to her, and stood looking down into the drawer, as she was looking down. Mesmerized, as she was, by what we saw.

Suddenly, there was evidence.

CHAPTER XVII

'THERE MUST BE some mistake,' Lou-Ann said desperately. 'There's got to be.'

Maw Cooney's handbag lay at the bottom of the drawer. We had all seen it too often, been made too aware of it, to mistake it.

Not one of us said anything. It was as though voicing our identification would be too positive, too final.

'But, what is it doing here?' Having admitted it to herself, Lou-Ann struggled with the next point. 'The police said somebody must've stolen it at the time of the accident. What is it doing in with Bart's things?'

It was a question no one wished to answer. The Cousins, drawn like vultures to the scene of catastrophe, came into the room, followed by Uncle No'ccount. Their grins fell away as they looked down into the drawer. For once, they seemed to recognize that some situations were beyond sniggering at.

'Maybe it ain't really hers,' Cousin Homer suggested tentatively. 'Maybe it jest *looks* the same.'

'You think I don't know my own Maw's bag?' Galvanized by the idea, Lou-Ann snatched up the bag and opened it.

'Looky here.' She began pulling out the contents,

tossing them on the dressing-table top. 'That's *her* wallet, *her* notebook, *her* set of publicity pictures of me, *her*—' Lou-Ann broke off, staring in puzzlement at the little bottle of pills she found in her hand.

'That's funny,' she said, '*these* ain't hers.' She dropped them on the dressing-table.

'They sure ain't!' Cousin Zeke moved forward and picked up the bottle. 'They's mine! They's what Bart took away from me on the boat. He told me he threw them overboard.'

Not all of them caught the implications at the same time. I saw Crystal move closer to Uncle No'ccount and receive his sheltering arm—they had had more experience of Bart's malice than the others. They were under no illusions as to his capabilities.

'*Your* sleeping pills.' Sam came to it reluctantly, but inescapably, almost with relief. It meant goodbye to the big plans the Agency had had for Bart—this meant he was too much dynamite even for them to handle. But it also meant Lou-Ann had been telling the truth when she swore she hadn't attempted suicide.

'For sure, they're mine. Jest you look at the label on that bottle—Dr H. D. Cadwallader, of Macon, Georgia. You remember.' He turned to the other Cousins for confirmation. 'We was playing a split week there when I was took so bad. He gave me some of those, and they helped so much I got him to do me a prescription for this tour. Ain't that so?'

They nodded agreement. Whatever else was murky, that much was clear. They remembered that split week in Macon, they remembered Dr H. D. Cadwallader—and the pills were definitely Zeke's.

'HYE!' the blurred, enraged voice from the bed startled us. 'You damn trash—what you doin' with my things?' Bart stumbled out of bed and towards us. 'You leave my things alone—you hear me?'

'They ain't your things, Bart.' Lou-Ann faced him calmly, but her voice quavered. 'They're Maw's.'

'And mine,' Zeke said, then retreated before Bart's furious glare.

'Give me that!' Bart snatched at the handbag.

Lou-Ann did not retreat. She held the bag tightly. 'It's Maw's, Bart. She always had it with her. It's the one the police couldn't find after she'd been hit by that car.'

Bart may have been groggy, but his sense of self preservation was still operating. Intimidation hadn't worked, so he switched on his most charming smile. 'You're upset, honey,' he said tenderly. 'Jest give me that now, and we'll talk about it later.'

Perhaps that smile had done something to Lou-Ann once, but the magic wasn't working any more. 'We can talk about it now,' she said.

The smile slowly faded from his face, but he kept a pleasant expression, the smile ready to make a comeback if there were any chance of it doing any good. He shook his head groggily and put a hand up to rub it; but, if that was a bid for sympathy, it failed, too. Lou-Ann regarded him impassively.

'The police told us it must've been stolen,' she said. 'So how come you've got it, Bart?'

We were all watching him, but it was Lou-Ann he must face and try to answer. He wasn't doing so well.

'Honey.' He rubbed his forehead again, touched the back of his head gingerly, and winced. 'Honey, I feel so awful. You got the doctor comin' for me?'

'He'll come.' There was a quality in her tone that

said someone else might come for Bart, too. In fact, there was a new quality about her entirely—a steely coldness, coupled with a rigid control. She was changing before our eyes, and what we could see was only part of what was happening deep inside her. Perhaps she was growing up.

'It was like this,' Bart tried again. 'After the police told us what happened—and everything—I went down to sorta have a look around where it happened. And I found this flung in the bushes, like, and—'

It wasn't good enough, and he knew it. But he went on trying.

'So naturally I brought it back, and I was afeared it might upset you, if you saw it, so I didn't—'

'Why didn't you give it to the police?' Lou-Ann asked.

'Why, I couldn't do that, honey.' He sounded surprised. 'I mean, there mighta been something in it we wouldn't want for them to see.'

That, at least, had a ring of truth. The first truth in the whole farrago. Maw Cooney had been ruling his life by blackmail. When he killed her, he had to take her handbag away to obtain any evidence she might have been carrying. Whether there had been anything or not, we would never know.

'After you checked, then why didn't you give it to the police? You knew they were looking for it.'

'Aw, honey, I couldn't do a thing like that to you. It would've jest started them coming back around again, asking lots more questions, stirring it all up again. You don't realize jest how upset you was. I couldn't have you bothered no more.'

'I know how upset I was, Bart,' Lou-Ann said quietly. 'I was mighty upset. But I wasn't near so crazy with it as you tried to make out to everybody. Now, why was that, I wonder?'

'Honey, I swear to you, you *was* that upset. Why, I was truly afeared—' But he had gone too far into another danger zone. He saw that, and stopped abruptly.

'No, Bart,' Lou-Ann said sadly. 'I wasn't *that* upset. Maw wouldn't have wanted for me to be. And I know how many pills I took that night, too. I only took one. And I hid the bottle so's you couldn't find it and throw them away, like you done Zeke's.' She paused, and corrected herself. 'Like we thought you done Zeke's.'

'Honey.' He was shaking his head, still protesting, but the verdict was going against him. The watching faces had closed against him.

'Zeke—' Lou-Ann gestured to the bottle—'you said you had enough pills for the tour. You know jest how many you had left?'

'Sure do, Lou-Ann. I had exactly thirty-six.'

'Thirty-six,' Lou-Ann said thoughtfully. 'Suppose you count them right now, and see how many you got there.'

'Sure, Lou-Ann.' She was calm, but Zeke's hand was trembling slightly as he spilled the pills across the dressing-table and pawed through them, counting aloud . . .

'. . . twenty-eight . . . twenty-nine . . . thirty . . . thirty-one . . . thirty-two . . .' He ran his hand frantically over the dressing-table, searching for some that might have rolled out of sight. There were none, of course. He turned to face her slowly.

'I make it thirty-two, Lou-Ann,' he announced. 'But I *know* there was thirty-six last time I had that bottle.'

'I expect there were, Zeke,' Lou-Ann said wearily. She looked at Bart and shrugged.

Incredibly, I had to swallow hard against a rising bubble of laughter in my throat. She was lost, sad, forlorn. But she was also brilliantly, exquisitely funny.

'What're you tryin' to say?' Bart reverted to bluster. He glared from one to the other. 'What kinda stupid put-up job is this?'

His day was over. Nobody cringed. But there was nothing funny now.

'I jest took one pill that night,' Lou-Ann said. 'So you must've given me the other four in that cocoa. Did you think that five would be enough? I expect it didn't matter, did it?' She sighed. 'You still had plenty in that bottle—and nobody would've been so surprised next time it happened.' She didn't look at him. She never looked at him again.

'Okay, Bart.' Sam snapped into life. 'Pack your things and get out of here. I don't care where you go— just go. You are finished, boy. Don't ever come near us or the Agency again.'

'You can't believe *her*,' Bart protested. 'She's jealous, that's all. She's so crazy mad, she reckons if she can't have me, then—'

'Do you think you could convince the police of that?' I asked.

'You, boy!' He turned on me, lowering his head like a bull about to charge. 'You've had it in for me from the beginning. And I ain't so hot on you, neither.' He was maddened with fury and terror. Somehow, he had decided that I was responsible for everything that had gone wrong for him since he had landed in this country.

'You and me, boy—' he all but pawed the ground— 'are gonna have it out right *now*.' He rushed at me in a demented charge.

He'd never heard of the Marquess of Queensberry. Or, if he had, he thought such stupid Rules only applied to the sissified English, and not to red-blooded jest plain folks.

His charge slammed me against the farther wall. He kidney-punched me with one hand and gouged for my eyes with the other.

I said goodbye to the Marquess myself and brought my knee up. We were too close for it to do much damage, but he released me briefly and I tried to get away. I had no illusions about my chances in a prolonged stand-up fight with Bart.

'You wanna fight dirty, boy—okay!' He leaped at me again. I heard the window-pane crack as my head slammed against it.

I was fighting as hard as I could, but I might as well have been swimming under water in slow motion. Vaguely, I wondered why no one was trying to help me. Would it have violated their Code of the Hills? Or, from where they stood, could it look as though I was holding my own?

Iron bands closed around my throat and blood filmed my eyes. If he had been satisfied to stand still and keep tightening those hands, Bart would have added me to his victims. But he jostled me along, muttering curses, shaking me like a terrier.

We careened back and forth along the wall, and I tried to keep punching—always hoping to land a lucky blow.

Then suddenly, the wall gave way, and we were leaning perilously out into space. Some damned fool had thoughtfully opened the window so that we wouldn't break it.

Bart loosened his hold while we both scrabbled for balance. For an instant, I was completely free of him, and aware of friendly hands pulling me back into the room.

Through the haze of blood filming my eyes, I had the dim impression of other hands clutching Bart, who thrashed about, still snarling curses. He must have hit the window-frame, the window started to slide down, and then—

I couldn't see properly, I was still gasping for breath, all I had was a dim impression of movement.

With a choked cry, Bart disappeared. The window crashed down with a violence that broke the glass. Was I imagining things, or had one pair of those 'helping' hands actually pushed?

There was silence in the room, except for the last shards of glass tinkling to the floor. We were all lost in our private thoughts. Or were we getting our stories straight?

'Poor guy,' Sam said finally, 'he hadn't been feeling well all day. He'd already had one dizzy spell in the dressing-room, when he fell and hit his head. And then, the window hitting him like that—when he just leaned out for a breath of air—'

'Too bad,' Uncle No'ccount said. 'I suppose maybe we ought to call the police. Seems like they'll have to know.'

Cousin Zeke carefully pushed the pills back into the bottle and put it in his pocket. 'Reckon maybe they'll already know,' he said. 'Seems to be a powerful lot of commotion down there.'

Lou-Ann just sobbed. Crystal put her arm around her waist and led her into the sitting-room. There was nothing anyone else could do for her.

They were all looking at me, I realized. Waiting.

What, after all, had I actually seen? There was only

the split second impression of hands lashing out. I couldn't even say whose hands.

You can't stand up in court and swear to an impression. That isn't evidence.

'This has been . . . a very sad tour . . . for all of you . . .' I said slowly. 'I hope . . . you won't take away entirely unhappy memories . . . of our country.' I could feel relaxation in the air around me.

'I'm sure,' I continued, 'you will all . . . manage to rise above these unhappy events . . . and go on to greater heights.'

Sam came round to the office on the morning of the day they were flying back. He brought the new pilot film along and insisted on showing it to us. It came out rather strangely against the green distempered walls of the office but, even with that drawback, we could see that he really had something.

They had rethought the entire script, scrapping the original concept completely. Now Lou-Ann was the star, backed by her friend and buddy, 'The Non-Feudin' Hatfield'—a toothily smiling Eugene, Uncle No'ccount behind him for ever, and with full credit for the songs. The dentist had done a magnificent job, giving him a set with just that hint of buck-toothed unevenness to make them look genuine.

But that was nothing to the change in Lou-Ann. She was smooth, relaxed—and brilliantly funny. She could throw a line away with the best of them now. Tossing it languidly over her shoulder, as though she didn't care whether you caught it or not. Perhaps she didn't.

The new, bright, hard quality was still in evidence.

Although she was smart enough to learn to hide that as time went on.

'How are things going, otherwise?' I asked Sam.

'Just swell.' He didn't pretend to misunderstand. 'It's much too early, of course. But she agrees, in principle. We—' he was suddenly shy—'we're going home for Christmas with the family.'

'That's fine.' If I was a trifle hearty, he didn't notice. His mother could welcome a poor little widow with a welcome a divorcée would never have received. Things were changing in the world—but not that much—not among the old families.

I looked at the film again. Lou-Ann, unhampered by a doorknob passing through her wrist, was tossing off a line with an airy gesture. It was the line she usually took a pratfall on.

Sam had his great comedienne. Bright, funny, and uncaring. Whether he would ever again find the woman beneath was his problem—and he was welcome to it. He didn't seem to have any doubts.

We parted warmly. Sam's handshake was made even warmer by the folded slip of paper in his hand. 'A bonus,' he explained. 'You'll be getting the bill after it's been cleared by the Home Office, but this is extra—and they agreed. You boys have really done a great job handling this tour.'

It was all very civilized. Who was I to bring up a nasty word like 'bribe'? We exchanged several protestations of mutual undying affection, then Sam went off.

'Have to collect Lou-Ann,' he said. 'She's got a last couple of errands before we leave.' He waved, and went down the stairs.

Gerry and I exchanged glances. I tossed the cheque

on the desk. Somehow, neither of us felt like looking at it. We knew the Agency would have done the right thing by us. We were in the black. We were solvent again. Now all we wanted was something to take the bitter taste out of our mouths.

Gerry slumped down on the edge of the desk, staring moodily out the window. He made no move when the telephone rang, so I answered it.

A crisp Kensington voice crackled at me imperiously. After a moment, I could even make out what she was saying. I put my hand over the receiver and motioned to Gerry.

'Do we want to handle a cat show?' I asked.

'A cat-house?' Gerry brightened perceptibly.

'Only in the broader sense,' I said. 'A Cat Show. You know, Best of Breed, and all that sort of thing.'

'Oh, hell.' Gerry slumped back on to the desk. 'Why not? It will make a change to *admit* our clients are four-footed.'

I turned back to the phone and agreed with the Kensington canary that a cat show was just the sort of clean-living, right-thinking account Perkins & Tate (Public Relations) Ltd would be delighted to handle. It should have been the truth.

Why then did I suddenly feel that I had just been sold a pup?

If you enjoyed COVER-UP STORY by Marian Babson, you won't want to miss her next exciting Bantam mystery, UNTIMELY GUEST.

The following is a preview of UNTIMELY GUEST, available from Bantam Books in January, 1992.

To BEGIN with, there were the questions—not one of which she could, hand on heart, answer with any degree of certitude.

'Will she have any hair?' Nicholas kept asking urgently during the long days of waiting. At seven, certain questions acquired an importance disproportionate to their intrinsic value. Part of it, Eleanor suspected, was based on their annoyance quotient to adult figures of authority. 'Will she have any hair at all?'

'Don't be silly, Nicholas.' A calm tone, an unruffled appearance—try to minimize the situation, make it appear part of the normal flow of life. 'Of course she will.' (Dear God, *would* she?)

'But how much hair will she have?' Nicholas persisted. 'And will it be real hair, like yours? Or will it be just all stubby, like Daddy when he needs a shave?'

'Go and wash your hands. We'll be eating soon.'

'Mickey Concannon says she'll be bald as an egg. He says that's why girls go in to begin with—so that nobody will notice.'

'Wash your hands!'

Kevin, thirty years older than Nicholas—but not, apparently, old enough to know better—began on his own leitmotive as he came through the door.

'How long is she going to stay?'

'How should I know? You read the only letter she sent. You know as much about it as I do.'

'I'm sorry,' His contrition didn't extend to changing the subject. 'If only we had some idea of her plans. Do you think she's going to be here a few days? A few weeks? She couldn't think we mean her to move in permanently, could she?'

'I don't know.'

'I wonder, was it wise? I know we've got the spare room, but—?'

It's always fatal to decide upon the last thing one ought to say to a loved one in any given situation. When that situation arises, there's the thing right on the tip of your tongue. She heard herself hurl it at him now.

'She's *your* sister!'

'I know, I know.' He was immediately defensive, taking it as a criticism. 'But she couldn't go home. Veronica has enough to cope with. We'll be lucky if this doesn't kill Mam, as it is. She'll never be able to understand.'

Her father had gone on private record, at the stormy time of their wedding, with his opinion that Mam was a woman you couldn't kill with a meat-axe. But it was not the sort of remark calculated to endear a daughter-in-law, if repeated.

'Times are changing,' she temporized. 'Mam will just have to learn that.'

'Ah,' he shook his head. 'But *will* she?'

The telephone saved her from having to answer that one.

'Hello? Ellie, is that you?' Carmel's voice came bubbling over the wire.

'Hello, Carmel.' Eleanor resisted the temptation to say, *'No, it's Bridie,'* and hear Carmel's gasp of consternation.

'Has she come yet?' The conspiratorial tone was somehow out of place when one considered that Carmel phoned at least three times a day to ask the same question.

'I told you I'd ring you when she arrived.' That, too, had been said many times before.

'I know. But she might have just come and you might not have been able to get to the phone yet.' Carmel's life was a succession of improbable speculations, none the less real to her for being engendered by the magic word 'might'. Anything *might* happen. Perhaps it helped to inure her to the fact that all that *did* happen—with monotonous regularity—was pregnancy.

'Well, she hasn't.'

'Do you suppose she might have changed her mind?'

'That would be too much to hope for.' The best thing about Carmel was that one could be honest with her and know that she'd understand. Outwardly unlike, Eleanor and Carmel had a bond no man could put asunder—they had both married into the same family. Consequently, they were the only members of it capable of standing back and watching with some degree of detachment when internecine warfare threatened to overwhelm all up to and including the third degree of kinship.

'I thought I might come round later—if you're going to be home.'

'I'll be here,' Eleanor agreed, ringing off. Carmel had learned as much as she had called to find out.

Passing the high chair in which Margaret perched docilely chewing a rusk, Eleanor caressed the soft feathery curls. It would be months yet before Margaret learned to talk. She was literally incapable of asking questions. At the moment, that made her Eleanor's favourite member of the family.

Upstairs, the spare room waited. Eleanor stood in the doorway, checking it automatically. (What did she expect to find? That Bridie had moved in unnoticed and taken up residence?)

Tomorrow the flowers would need changing. She knew that Kevin thought it a useless gesture to keep the vases filled in an empty room, but she could not bear the thought that Bridie might arrive without any further warning and find no slightest sign of welcome waiting for her. Bridie had so little to come back to.

She moved into the room, hovering irresolutely. Did it look all right? The mirror—should it really be in the room at all? There was already one mirror—part of the dressing-table—was the second one, hanging on the wall, too much? But, if she took it down, she had nothing to replace it and the long narrow swatch of unfaded wallpaper would proclaim what was missing as surely as if it had been labelled. Mirrors have such a distinctive shape.

But the Victorian *prie-dieu* squatting against the farther wall was the basic source of her uneasiness. Should she—she went over the familiar ground again—leave it in the room? Would Bridie take it as some sort of personal comment? Or, if she moved it out into the hall, would Bridie bring it back in here?

It was the sort of small problem that had grown to enormous size and insolubility during the past few days. (Kevin didn't know. 'Heavens, don't ask *me*,' Carmel had shuddered. Veronica had withdrawn so far into the fastnesses of her own life and troubles that it seemed unkinder to risk upsetting her than upsetting Bridie.)

Eleanor closed her eyes, trying to recall Bridie to mind, but it had been ten years ago. She had just started going with Kevin and his family were still shadowy figures in the distance whom it might not be necessary for her ever to meet. He hadn't even talked about them much. Not until that sudden upsurge of drama, during which one sister ran away with another's fiancé, their father died in pursuit of the elopers, and the jilted sister retreated completely from a life which had become too much for her. (Kevin had reluctantly imparted the information, obviously feeling that his wife-to-be was going to have to know a few things about the family.)

It was about the same time that Patrick had proposed to Carmel, and the weddings of the two sons, following so closely on one another, had tended to obscure the earlier drama. Besides, Bridie had been so neatly—fittingly—out of the way by then that she was regarded by most of the family as having almost decently been buried. Who would have imagined that she would snap back into life again all these years later?

Eleanor moved the *prie-dieu* away from the wall, setting it beside the bed. Did it look more like an ordinary chair there? (It didn't look in any way *reproachful*, did it?) She might have put it somewhere else, but it had always been in the guest-room and Nicholas would be sure to comment upon it—unfailingly at the wrong moment. (Could there be any *right* moment?) Or Bridie might see it, wherever she put it, and to have such a chair in the house, but not in Bridie's room, would seem more pointed than leaving it here.

The doorbell rang—that would be Carmel. With a final desperate glare at the *prie-dieu*, Eleanor pushed it slightly askew (as though a more rakish angle might somehow disguise it) and hurried downstairs.

There was a howl from the kitchen as she reached the foot of the stairs.

'Mother—' Nicholas's indignant bellow filled the hallway. 'Margaret threw her milk at me. It's all over the floor.'

'And what did you do to her to—?' Eleanor flung the front door ajar in passing, bellowing back preparatory to joining the battle in the kitchen. It was highly unlikely that Margaret had deliberately thrown her milk at Nicholas. It was far more likely that she had spilled it, or that he had knocked it over teasing her. That the milk was all over the floor was the only point in his statement she didn't doubt.

Almost to the kitchen, she halted. There

were no following footsteps—as there would have been had Carmel entered. And, come to think of it, the brief glimpse she had had of the slight form in the doorway had shown no resemblance to Carmel.

'Oh God!' She did an abrupt about-face and retraced her steps.

The figure stood waiting, eyes cast down, hands folded at waist, the two suitcases at her side nearly as big as she was—certainly a lot bulkier.

'*Do* come in!' Eleanor opened the door wide. 'I'm so sorry, I thought it was—I mean, I wasn't expecting—Come in—' (*What* did one call her?)

'No, please—' As the slight figure stooped to take up the suitcases, Eleanor stopped her. 'Kevin will see to those.' She raised her voice above the din coming from the kitchen. 'Kevin! KE-vin!'

Then he was behind her, uneasy, cued by the faint note of hysteria in her voice.

'Bridie!' He put his hand out, then seemed to realize that that was a bit too formal a greeting for a sister.

As Bridie, with delayed reaction, unclasped her hands and started to hold one out, Kevin bobbed to plant a kiss on her cheek. They collided awkwardly.

'The cases,' Eleanor said.

'Of course.' Kevin gathered them up, grateful for something to do. 'Of course. I'll take them upstairs.' He escaped thankfully.

The uproar in the kitchen had not abated. Margaret had begun to cry and Nicholas was issuing a lurid up-to-the-second bulletin at the top of his lungs every thirty seconds.

'Mother—Margaret's got a puddle of milk on her tray and she's hitting it with her hand . . . Mother—she's splattering it everywhere! . . . Mother—Margaret's making faces at me . . . Mother—Margaret's crying!'

'I know. We can hear her.' Eleanor fought down the temptation to go and smack them both. Why did children always play up as soon as guests arrived? She glanced at Bridie sympathetically, ready to meet her eyes with a rueful shrug.

Bridie's eyes remained resolutely downcast, but she could not hide a flinch as she crossed the doorstep and the din from the kitchen engulfed her.

Bridie would just have to get used to it, Eleanor decided. At that, it was several decibels below the racket produced when any of Carmel's brood joined her own. Bridie would never again, in all likelihood, find a place as quiet as the place she had left. Bridie would simply have to adjust—toughen up—like everybody else in the world.

An inhospitable little thought—perhaps triggered off by the spring in Kevin's step as he bounded up the stairs—snaked through her mind. If Bridie found the atmosphere uncongenial here, perhaps she wouldn't stay long.

Poor Bridie, Eleanor reproached herself instantly. *After all she must have been through. How can you—?*

'Mother!' Unable to raise any satisfactory response to his urgent bellowing, Nicholas charged into the hallway to see what the rival attraction was. He stopped short, staring at Bridie. 'Oh!'

Eleanor was profoundly grateful that Bridie *did* have hair. A bit short, perhaps, but *there*. Not that that would necessarily prevent Nicholas from commenting just the same.

'Nicholas,' she said hastily, before he got his breath back. 'This is your Aunt Bridget. Say hello to her—like a gentleman.'

'Hello.' The warning in his mother's voice would be disregarded at his future peril and he knew it. He produced his sweetest smile as added insurance.

Eleanor allowed herself to relax for a moment—perhaps it wasn't going to be so bad, after all. If Nicholas decided to behave . . . If Kevin would stop jittering . . .

Then she looked at her guest. Bridie was rigid with an emotion that might have been fear—but only partly fear. Fear, one could sympathize with and understand. It was the other emotion that repelled Eleanor.

Bridie's face was a mask of cold distaste. Her eyes, as she looked at Nicholas, were filled with a loathing she could not disguise. Perhaps she realized this; she lowered her lids quickly, nodded to a dismayed Nicholas, and stood there in a meek submissive pose which could fool no one who had suddenly had a glimpse of the cauldron bubbling just below the surface.

Eleanor knew then that this visitation was going to be far worse—far, far bloodier—than she had ever feared.

At Annie Laurance's Death on Demand bookstore, murder is often more than just a reading experience and the mysteries are just leaping off the shelves.

CAROLYN HART

Carolyn Hart's Annie and Max are two of mystery readers' best loved characters and in these award-winning books you'll join them on their adventures of mystery, danger and several volumes of murder most foul.

BANTAM OFFERS THE FINEST IN CLASSIC AND MODERN BRITISH MURDER MYSTERIES

Dorothy Cannell
❑	The Widows Club	27794-4	$3.95
❑	Down the Garden Path	26895-3	$3.95
❑	Mum's the Word	28686-2	$4.99

Michael Dibdin
❑	Ratking	28237-9	$4.99

Colin Dexter
❑	The Dead of Jericho	27237-3	$3.95
❑	Last Bus to Woodstock	27777-4	$3.95
❑	Last Seen Wearing	28003-1	$3.95
❑	The Riddle of the Third Mile	27363-9	$4.50
❑	The Silent World of Nicholas Quinn	27238-1	$3.95
❑	Service of All the Dead	27239-X	$3.95
❑	The Secret of Annex 3	27549-6	$3.95

Dorothy Simpson
❑	Close Her Eyes	18518-7	$2.25
❑	Dead by Morning	28606-4	$3.95
❑	Dead on Arrival	27000-1	$3.50
❑	Element of Doubt	28175-5	$3.50
❑	Last Seen Alive	27773-1	$3.95
❑	Night She Died	27772-3	$3.50
❑	Puppet for a Corpse	27774-X	$3.95
❑	Six Feet Under	25192-9	$3.95
❑	Suspicious Death	28459-2	$3.95

Available at your local bookstore or use this page to order.

Send to: Bantam Books, Dept. MC 6
414 East Golf Road
Des Plaines, IL 60016

Please send me the items I have checked above. I am enclosing
$_____ (please add $2.50 to cover postage and handling).
Send check or money order, no cash or C.O.D.'s, please.

Mr/Ms._____

Address_____

City/State_____Zip_____

Please allow four to six weeks for delivery.
Prices and availability subject to change without notice.   MC6 11/91